For Adele Tillson
a happy birthday

CONTENTS

The Young in Heart

"SHE ATE GRASS?"

✿✿✿✿ The boy with the somber face walked into the Island Market and began turning out his pockets. He pulled out the two side pockets of his white duck pants and then fished in the breast pocket of his white shirt, which was unbuttoned, the tails knotted about his waist. "Now where the hell'd I put it?" he said.

"Put what?" his friend Angie, in dungarees and barefoot, asked him.

"Here it is," he said, and pulled the slip of paper out of his hip pocket. "Look," he said to Angie, "you go over and order the booze, I'm going to look in Gourmet Foods."

"Gourmet *foods?*" Angie said.

"Yeah. Get three bottles of bourbon. Make it four bottles of bourbon." He walked toward the aisle marked "Gourmet Foods," and Angie walked over to the liquor department.

Two ladies, both in shorts and squashed-looking sneakers, and both on the critical list at Weight Watchers, were in a hypnotic trance over the items of Gourmet Foods, lifting cans from the shelves, shaking them, inspecting labels, and putting the cans back. The boy hovered behind them for a moment or two, peer-

3

ing over their shoulders, making a humming, buzzing noise between his teeth.

"You want to get in here?" one woman asked, turning to
him.

"No, thanks." He scooted down the aisle toward Bakery
Items.

When he rejoined Angie at the liquor counter he had a box
of cookies and two frozen candy bars. "Here," he said to the
clerk, "add these in."

He looked at what Angie had ordered. "Hell, man. She
doesn't like that cheap stuff. Is that what you buy? She likes
that good stuff. Over there. Four bottles," he said to the clerk,
who removed the bottles and replaced them.

"That be all?"

The boy nodded.

The clerk ran up the total on the tape, added in the cookies
and the candy bars, and presented the tape to the somber-faced
boy, who inspected it, humming buzzingly. Then he took the
folded check out of his pocket, flattened it, and picked up the
black ball-point pen that lay on the counter. The check was
printed with his mother's name, Alice C. Amis, and she had
already signed it, dated it and made it payable to "Island Market, Inc." The boy filled in the amount from the tape—$25.90
—and gave the check to the clerk, who examined it, made a
cryptic scribble on the back, and put it into his cash drawer.

Angie picked up the heavy paper bag, and the two boys
walked out of the store. It was afternoon. Opening the car door,
the dark-faced boy slid into the driver's seat, and Angie got in
beside him, placing the paper bag between them. The dark boy
reached into the bag, took out the candy bars and gave one to

Angie. Then hitching himself forward in the seat he dug his hands into the side pockets of his trousers and pulled out two more frozen candy bars. He winked and handed one of these to Angie too. "Played a little five-finger grab," he said, poking Angie in the shoulder.

"Hey, man!" Angie said, and laughed, and poked him back. For a moment the boys threw soft punches at each other in the front seat. Then the dark boy started the car.

He drove well and cautiously. After all, he would not be sixteen for two months, and the cops on the island were known to be rough about this sort of thing if they caught you. He stuck carefully to the speed limit; in fact, kept a little under it to be on the safe side.

"You going to the beach party tonight?" Angie asked him.

"I don't know."

"If you come, bring a bottle of booze," Angie said.

"How can I do that?"

Angie patted the paper bag. "Bring a bottle of this stuff."

"How can I do that?"

"You mean she'd notice?"

"Hell, yes, she'd notice. What do you think? I mean, she *notices.*"

Angie was silent for a moment, and then he said, "But what I mean is—well, if she's having a cocktail party and all—I mean, she's having the cocktail party *now,* isn't she? And, well, by nine or ten o'clock, if she's had a few drinks and all, do you think she'd notice if you snuck a bottle out? I mean—well, you know how it is. I don't think she'd even notice."

"Hell!" the boy said. "What do you think she *is,* anyway? I tell you she'd *notice.*"

"Don't get mad. I just meant it might be worth a try; that's all. No need to get mad about it."

"I don't even know if I'm going to *go* to the damn beach party."

"Anyway, Simmons says he's going to try to bring some booze," Angie said.

The boy said nothing. They drove in silence for a while, the boy's hands resting on the top of the steering wheel.

"Hey, where'd you get the neat ID bracelet?" Angie asked.

He showed Angie the silver bracelet on his tanned wrist. "This? My dad sent it to me. Like it?"

"Neat," Angie said. He fingered the heavy silver tag, flipped it over. "It's got no name on it. How come you don't have your name on it?"

The boy pulled his wrist away. "Hey! Don't grab my arm while I'm driving, you idiot! You want me to have an accident?"

"Sorry. I just meant—"

"I guess my dad didn't get around to getting it engraved," he said. "I mean, I guess engraving takes like a couple of weeks, and I guess he wanted me to have it right away. It's sterling silver. I guess I'd better get it engraved one of these days—have my name put on it, you know. And maybe my blood type? If I can find out what the hell my blood type is, I guess maybe I ought to have that put on it too; don't you think? I mean, like if something happens. A thing like that makes sense, and you never can tell. Know what I mean?"

Angie nodded. "Sure," he said.

"I've really been meaning to have that done," the boy said. "It's a neat bracelet."

"Sterling silver. I guess—oh, I guess it probably set my dad back twenty or thirty bucks; don't you think? At least."

"Too bad it doesn't have your name on it."

"Hell, I just *told* you I'm going to have my name put on it. I've been meaning to, in fact."

"Are your folks really going to get a divorce?" Angie asked him.

He nodded. "Uh-huh." He drove with one hand on the wheel now, and with his free hand he was unwrapping one of the candy bars.

"Well," Angie said, "I suppose they have to do it. My mother and dad did it, you know. They've been divorced—I don't know how long. It works out pretty well."

"Yes," the other boy said, nodding again. "It works out. It really does. I mean, right now, you see, my brother David is with my dad, and that works out. I mean, he and my dad get along pretty well. And I'm with Mom. And then when David comes to see Mom, then I'll go to see Dad, and it all works out. Yes," he said, his face grave, "it's the only answer, I guess. It makes sense. In the long run," he said, nodding soberly, "it's best."

He bit hard into the frozen candy bar, guiding the car expertly with his other hand, and said, "But—if only—" And then a queer thing happened. Two obstinate and totally unexplained tears sprang into his eyes, and for a moment the road before him blurred and he heard his right front tire spit angrily into the sand of the shoulder.

"Hey, watch it!" Angie said. "To hell with the one-arm driving, man. Cop'll give you a ticket for that."

"Sorry. My hand slipped."

Angie began a long account of an accident that had occurred two nights before, on the North Road, when a girl they both knew, driving a borrowed Thunderbird, had struck a stone wall, causing considerable damage to the front end of the car but no injuries to anyone. Angie had been one of the people in the car, and he described the accident in full detail—what had occurred immediately before, what had caused the girl to turn her head to say something to someone in the back seat, how the car had reacted, the kind of skid marks that had been left on the pavement, and what the girl's behavior had been like afterward. The dark-faced boy listened.

"She ate grass?" he asked suddenly.

"Man, she was hysterical. I mean, you can't blame her. It wasn't her T-bird. It belonged to the people she was sitting for, and the man had let her borrow it. But she wasn't supposed to be taking anybody for rides in it. She sort of went crazy! Hysterical. Got down on her hands and knees by the side of the road and started stuffing grass in her mouth! We kept saying to her, 'Look, you'll only have to pay for the fifty-dollar deductible. The insurance'll pay for the rest.' But she sat there screaming, 'Kill me! Kill me!' and stuffing grass in her mouth. I mean the things some people do are crazy."

The dark boy nodded, agreeing.

As he came to Angie's driveway, he slowed the car and pulled it off the road. "Well, be seeing you around, Ange," he said.

"See you at the beach party tonight maybe?"

"Maybe, I don't know."

"Well," Angie said, opening the door, "be seeing you."

"Take it easy." Angie started to get out and his friend said quickly, "Ange—when your parents got their divorce—"

"Yeah?" Angie said. "What about it?"

"Never mind. Skip it. So long, Ange." Angie got out, and the dark boy started the car again and drove toward home.

He turned slowly into his own driveway, drove up the hill, and parked in the circle before the house. He sat behind the wheel for a moment, finishing his second candy bar, and licked his fingers. Then he got out of the car in an unusual way—unusual, that is, for most people, but not unusual for him; it was his customary way of disgorging himself from an automobile when he was alone. He went out the window, head first, sliding his body out, across the window's edge, feet braced against the ceiling of the car, until his hands touched the ground outside. Then he performed a handstand in the air, flipped backward onto his feet and stood up. When he was home, in the apartment in New York, he liked to ride up the elevator standing on his hands when he was alone. There was something about being alone in elevators and in cars that made you want to do unlikely things, but since there was never anyone to see you, these feats were always performed in a kind of void.

He reached back into the front seat of the car, lifted out the bag of liquor and walked up to the house.

The living room was filled with smoke and people, some reasonably famous faces, all of them reasonably familiar, his mother's friends.

"Ah, young Ganymede returns!" a woman's voice cried out to him. "Ganymede returns, come to replenish our empty cups! Quick, quick, we're dying of thirst."

His mother was in pale-blue silk slacks and silver shoes with wide, flat silver bows, and her face was flushed and smiling, and her dark, pretty eyes were misted from laughter. "Take the liquor into the kitchen, darling, will you?" she said.

As he crossed the living room toward the kitchen, a woman whose name he could not remember said to him, "Are you

David or are you John? You boys look so much alike I never can keep you straight!"

He stopped and smiled at her. "I'm David," John said.

"How you've grown!"

His mother followed him into the kitchen. "Thank you, darling," she said. "I take it you had no trouble at the store."

"Trouble? Why should I have trouble, Mom?"

"Because of your *age*, silly. Anyway, I phoned them and told them you'd be coming in for liquor." The boy placed the bag on the countertop, and his mother lifted the bottles out one by one and set them on the little bar. "You got nothing but bourbon!"

"It's the kind you like, isn't it, Mom?"

"Yes, but we have a few Scotch drinkers. But it doesn't matter. They won't notice the difference at this point."

She moved quickly and breathlessly back and forth across the kitchen, her silver heels clicking on the black-and-white tile squares that were laid out like a checkerboard. She returned to the living room, and her son stood in front of the kitchen sink. Thoughtfully he turned on the faucet, gazed for a moment at the thin silver icicle of water that poured out, then shut it off.

His mother appeared behind him, carrying a tray of empty glasses. "Mom," he said, "did you ever hear of anybody getting so upset about something that they got down on their hands and knees and ate *grass?*"

"Never," she said. "Oh, I forgot to tell you, darling. Your father called while you were out."

"What does he want?"

"How should *I* know? I didn't talk to him. The call was for you."

"But, gosh, Mom! Couldn't you at least have asked him what

he wanted? I mean, after all! It might have been something important!"

"If you're curious, dear, I'd suggest you call him back," she said.

He went to the telephone on the kitchen wall while his mother moved about, mixing drinks. He lifted the receiver and dialed Operator and gave her the New York number. Leaning against the wall he held the receiver to his ear with one hand and plugged his other ear with the other hand to block out the party noises from the living room. With the smooth tag of his identification bracelet he rubbed his cheek.

"Alice?" he heard someone call to his mother. "What are you going to do about August? Are you going to stay here?"

"Heavens!" he heard her answer. "I'm so pleased to have *July* worked out! Don't ask me where I'll be in August."

The boy listened intently to the operator's report. "There are a couple of other numbers where you might be able to reach him," he said. He gave her the other numbers and waited. "Let that number ring a long time, please," he said after a while. "He might be taking a nap, or something."

"I am ringing your number," the operator said.

"Would I like Acapulco?" he heard his mother ask. She was in the living room.

When his mother came back into the kitchen, he had hung up the phone and was just standing there. She said, "Did you get him, dear?"

"He's left the office, he's not at the club, and there's no answer at the apartment," he said.

"Well, perhaps you can try him later."

He reached inside the pocket of his shirt. "Here's the slip for the liquor, Mom."

"Oh, thank you, dear."

She opened the refrigerator door and removed a tray of ice cubes. She carried it to the sink and said, "Darling, will you take out these ice cubes for me?"

When there was no answer she turned and discovered that he was gone, evaporated into air.

So Alice Amis cracked open the ice tray herself and, using her fingers, dropped cubes into several glasses. From behind her a man's arms circled her waist, and she pushed him off with a laugh, saying, "Oh, behave yourself!"

"Where's your good-looking son?" he asked.

"Vanished!" she laughed. "He's always vanishing."

"How's he taking the divorce thing?"

"Seriously, I think both boys want me to be happy," she said.

The man wandered back into the living room, and she finished mixing the drinks and arranged the glasses on the tray. When the tray was ready, she started to lift it, hesitated, and put it down. She looked toward the living room where the party was, lifted the tray again, and once more set it down.

Alice Amis stood on tiptoe at the kitchen door as if balanced on the edge of something, as though the saddle of wood between the kitchen and the living room marked the top of a cliff, and her choice was whether to step forward, down into the clear possibilities that the living room contained, or return to the puzzle pattern of the kitchen tile. Her hand touched the doorjamb briefly. Then she turned. She felt herself walking back across the kitchen to the door of her son's room. It was meant to be a maid's room, but it was the room he had for some reason chosen in this rented summer house. The smallest bedroom in the place, he had insisted on making it his.

She heard her soft voice call, "John? John?" And then, a

little louder, "Johnnie? Johnnie?" She played a little rhythm on the panel of the door with her well-polished fingernails. Finally she tried the knob. But he had locked it from the other side, and was in there, and would not answer her.

CALL BEFORE DINNER

✵✵✵✵ When the telephone rang in the hotel room the young man who was lying, fully dressed, on one of the twin beds next to it, reached over and picked up the receiver in the middle of the first ring. "Hello?" he said.

"Mr. Edward Martin?"

"Yes."

"One moment, please, for Long Distance."

He waited, attempting to light a cigarette, cradling the phone between his ear and shoulder with difficulty, digging into the pocket of his gray slacks for matches.

"Hello?" he heard his mother's voice say. "Teddy? Is that you, Teddy?"

"Hi," he said. "How're you, Mom?"

"Fine," she said. "Have you had your dinner yet, Teddy?"

"No, not yet."

"Well," his mother said, "don't let me keep you from your dinner."

"Look," he said, "did you call me up two thousand miles to tell me it was time for dinner?"

14

"No, of course not, silly," she said. "I just don't want to delay your dinner, that's all. How are you?"

"Oh, I'm fine, Mom. Just fine."

"Oh, that's good. How's your room?"

"Fine. Just fine."

"I mean, what's it like? Does it have a balcony? I asked for a balcony."

"Yes, it's got a balcony."

"Do you have a view?"

He half turned as though he were not sure of the answer, and looked across the room to the French doors. "Yes," he said, "you can see practically the whole Caribbean from up here, I guess."

"Oh, that's nice. It must be pretty. How is—everything else?"

"What do you mean, everything else?"

"Well, you've been down there a week and Daddy and I have both written you. But we haven't gotten so much as a postcard from you. How *is* everything?"

"You mean—"

"I mean Carol, of course, yes."

The young man completed his turn now, and looked at the girl who occupied the other twin bed. She lay, in a wide, bright orange skirt, on top of the bed, looking up at the ceiling.

"Carol's fine," he said.

"Has she seen the doctor yet?"

"Yes."

"Did he mention any date?"

"Around the twenty-first of August," he said. "But Carol says it could be a week earlier or later."

"What else did he say?"

"That's all. She's fine. He's worried about her attitude, that's all."

"Her attitude? What's wrong with her attitude, for heaven's sake?"

"Oh, you know," he said softly. "It's been hard on her. The wedding. Everything."

"She should be thankful she had a wedding. What's her doctor like?"

"Nice," he said. "An Englishman."

"Oh, an Englishman, that's nice." There was a pause. "Teddy?"

"Yes, Mother?"

"Has she reached a decision yet?"

"What sort of a decision?" he asked.

"You know, Teddy. About the baby."

"No. She hasn't decided yet."

"Well, I do hope she is going to be sensible about it. Don't you, Teddy?"

"I don't know."

"You have all the papers there, don't you? The ones she has to sign for the adoption business?"

"Yes."

"Well, try to settle it, Teddy—once and for all—soon. Without any more hysterics. Histrionics, I mean. Under the circumstances it's unreasonable of her to want to keep the baby. I know her mother thinks so, too."

"Oh, have you talked to her?"

"I should say not. Goodness, it's impossible to talk to that woman. She gets hysterical over the phone every time I try to discuss anything sanely. No. All I can say is it's a good thing Daddy and I took things into our own hands, or heaven only knows where you'd both be." She paused. "By the way, dear, what are you doing about your laundry? Do you have plenty of shirts?"

"Yes, Mother," he said wearily. "Yes, Mother. Yes, Mother. Everything's fine."

"Teddy?" his mother said. "I talked to the Dean today. I told him the whole story. All about the little wedding and everything. He was very kind, terribly understanding. You can go back to college next fall if you make up your work this summer. Isn't that fine?"

There was a delay in his answering as he reached over and snapped on the lamp that stood on the night stand.

"Teddy?" his mother's voice said. "You didn't answer me about college. Do you want to go back next semester?"

"Sure," he said. "Sure. I guess I do."

"Oh, good! I'm glad. But you do see, don't you, how impossible—how unheard of—it would be for you to go back to college with some sort of baby in tow?"

"What do you mean 'some sort' of baby?"

"Don't get huffy, dear. You know what I mean. I mean it's just too much. You're not even twenty and you've two more years—more than two full years—of college ahead of you. You couldn't do that and be a parent, too, for heaven's sake!"

He made no reply.

"That's why the adoption is the only way. And as far as she's concerned, well, she can just go back to her family while you're in college."

"Yes," he said.

"And then—supposing you did decide to stay married to her—but you probably won't, because a divorce would be simple enough to arrange. I mean after this thing blows over—"

He turned, this time cautiously, and looked at the girl lying on the other bed. Slowly, without looking at him or getting up, she reached toward the other night stand on which lay a pack of cigarettes, matches, and an ashtray. She brought these closer to her, extracted a cigarette from the pack, and lighted it.

"Doesn't that make sense to you, Teddy? About not staying married to her? I mean, actually, why should you? I remember what you said—what you told me—that night. That night you gave us the news. You didn't want to marry her. You said so."

"Look, Mother," he said, "can we please skip all that?"

"Well," she said, "it's true. Don't you forget it. I'll never forget the expression on your face. And hers! Last week, at the wedding, at the lawyer's office. Did she look like a happy bride? Well, you're both lucky, that's all I can say, to have parents who can understand and afford to get the two of you married and packed off there to avoid the humiliation of a—a baby—arriving five months from now! And I hope you realize how much this little so-called honeymoon of yours is going to cost Daddy."

"Mother," he said, "look, we've had this conversation before. Do we have to go over it and over it?"

"No. I'm sorry," she said. "How's the weather been?"

He sighed. "The weather's fine."

"Have you taken any pictures?"

"What?"

"Pictures. You took your camera, didn't you?"

"No," he said. "No pictures."

"Well," his mother said, "I just hope she sees the sense of it. Goodness knows, there'll be questions—all the rest of her life—if she keeps that baby. And I just know that you don't care for her."

He said nothing.

"I mean, how could you?" she went on. "After all those years—going steady with her for—how long was it? Four and a half years? And not even a girl we approved of! And I warned you—"

"Mother!" he interrupted.

She stopped, and then suddenly said, "Teddy! *Is she in the room?*"

He looked at the girl who lay silently smoking. "Yes."

"Oh! Why didn't I think? Why didn't you tell me? Oh, I should have known, you've been acting so funny. Well," she said, "just answer me with yes and no. Would you like to talk to Daddy?"

"No," he said.

"Teddy, please. Don't be funny. Daddy's right here."

"I don't want to talk to him."

"Why not?"

"Because I don't. We had enough of talk—that night."

"Teddy, you know Daddy didn't mean some of those things he said. He didn't mean any of them. He was upset."

"I don't want to go through that again," he said.

"He didn't mean it, dear. That was just Daddy being—well, being Daddy! I mean, you know what great, what wonderful plans he had for you, dear. And it wasn't as if Daddy hadn't warned you—"

"I don't want to talk to him."

"Now, Daddy's right here, right at my shoulder, ready to talk to you. Now don't go flying off the handle with him, Teddy. Be nice. Remember that it's Daddy who's paying for all this and it isn't going to be exactly cheap. Now hold the wire and I'll put Daddy on."

"If you put him on, I'll hang up," he said.

But his mother had left the phone, and he did not hang up. Instead, he looked at the girl on the bed. His expression was embarrassed, somewhat imploring. She did not seem to see him, but lay, dry-eyed, holding her cigarette loose in one hand, with blue smoke trailing upward toward the ceiling.

Then his father's voice boomed halfway across the Caribbean. "Ted?" he said cheerfully. "How are you, boy?"

His voice filled the room and the girl turned toward the phone and listened with interest, her face grave and thoughtful.

"Fine, Dad."

"Good, good. Good to hear your voice, Son! I guess you talked to your mother."

He held the receiver an inch or so away from his ear. "We've got a good connection, haven't we?" he said.

"Yes. Well, you know your mother. She told the operator here not to bother placing the call unless she could promise us a good connection. How've you been?"

"Fine."

There was an awkward, suspended silence.

"Well, well," his father said. "How is everything?"

"Fine."

"You got those papers, didn't you? Those papers from the lawyer?"

"Yes, I did."

"Don't lose 'em, Ted. You know—all she needs to do is sign on the dotted line."

"Yes."

"And you tell her, Ted, that this agency *guarantees*—I mean they guarantee and triple guarantee to place that kid in a good home. She can rest absolutely assured that, no matter what, that baby will be placed in a good home. They guarantee it."

The young man said nothing.

"So you see," his father said, "there's nothing to worry about. You can tell her that. What's more, I talked to her old man and he agrees with me. Oh, I won't say it didn't take a little, ah, persuasion on my part to *get* him to agree. But he agreed."

The girl reacted to this by shutting her eyes and immediately opening them again.

"Say, he's a funny duck, don't you think? Her old man? You knew him, of course. Sure, you must have. But don't you think he's a funny duck? Well, I guess he was pretty upset, like we all were. He had some pretty plain and fancy things to say about you, as I guess you can imagine." His father laughed.

"I can imagine."

"Well, it'll all be over sooner than you can say Jack Robinson, and, like I always say, we live and learn, right?"

"Right."

"You've had your lesson. You had a good scare. And don't say I never warned you, Ted. But all that's water over the dam. In every sense of the word. Did your mother tell you she talked to Dean Willis?"

"Yes."

"Well, say, that's pretty good, huh? Back in school for the fall semester? Don't you think so?" There was a silence. The young man used it to fish another cigarette out of his pack and, struggling to hold phone, cigarette, and match book, finally got it lighted. During this, the girl on the other bed reached over and put her cigarette out in the ashtray with a series of slow taps. Then she sat up and brushed a lock of silky brown hair out of her eyes. She put her bare feet over the side of the bed and leaned over, searching for her shoes.

"Well, Son," his father said, "no hard feelings. I mean live and let live, okay? I mean you've learned your lesson. And you know darned good and well you couldn't go back to college trundling some teen-aged wife and kid. I mean it's out of the question and your own common sense should tell you that." He paused. "Just as long as she signs that paper, see? And the sooner the better. You asked her to, didn't you?"

"Yes."

"And what did she say? Look, if she's stalling around— look, I mean, see here, Ted, let me talk to her. Put her on the phone, will you? Let me talk some sense into her."

The girl found her shoes. They were white, made of canvas. She tied the laces carefully, then stood up. From the other bed, her husband turned and watched her.

"Ted? You hear me? Put her on the phone."

"No," he said. "No. Never mind that. I'll have her sign the paper. Don't worry."

"Well, all right, Son, if you think you can handle her," his father's voice said. "You do that and you'll be all right. Now here's your mother again. She wants to say good night. Good night, Son."

"Good night."

His mother's voice came on again, almost immediately. "Teddy," she said, "I'm afraid we've kept you talking way too long. Will you be late for dinner? I hope not. I want you to watch your meals. You remember what I told you about eating fresh vegetables in the tropics, though, won't you?"

"Yes, Mother."

"Good. Well, Teddy, good night now. Go down and have a nice dinner. And keep us posted, you know. Not just postcards, but letters. Or call. Call and reverse the charges."

"Yes, Mother." He watched as the girl crossed the room to

the French doors and stood, looking out into the night. She stood for several seconds, looking out, then opened one half of the French doors and stepped out onto the balcony. From the open door a warm tropical breeze blew into the room, stirring the smoke in the air. He watched her go to one of the two chaise longues—placed there for sunbathing—and sit down. Then, suddenly, the breeze drew the French door shut with a bang.

"What was that noise?" his mother asked.

"Carol just went out. The door shut."

"Oh, well, good. We can have a little last-minute privacy, then, can't we? Well, Teddy, I just want you to tell her—to be absolutely firm. To tell her that she *must* sign those papers and no two ways about it. You see, dear, what *really* worries Daddy —shall I tell you? What really worries Daddy is that she'll get the idea she can hold us up—for money. You know, use those papers as a threat, like blackmail."

He rested his cigarette on the edge of the night stand and reached up, and held the receiver now with two hands. He sat forward.

"Do you understand?"

"Mother," he said slowly, "listen to me for a minute."

"What?" she asked.

"Just listen. That's all. Listen! I've been listening to you for the past half hour and now you can damn well listen to me!"

"*Teddy!*"

"And stop calling me Teddy!"

"Teddy—"

"Stop it. Do you hear me? I'm not a baby, do you understand? Listen, I'm going to tell you just exactly what I've been thinking the whole time you've been talking, both of you!"

"Now see here, young man—"

"Quiet. Listen to me. I'm not a baby. Get that through your head. And Carol's not some cheap gold-digger, either. Look— maybe I hadn't decided, maybe I didn't know what I was going to do—up until now. But talking to you and Daddy—talking to you and *Father*—has sure helped me decide!"

"What are you talking about?"

"Shut up."

"Teddy!"

He stood up, holding the phone. "Listen here," he said. "Do you realize why we got in this mess? Do you? Do you know that for the whole four years we've gone together, Carol and I, you've never—not once—done anything? Not even so much as acknowledged her? You refused to get to know her, to meet her folks, to have her to dinner! You weren't even nice to her, you weren't even kind! And when I tried to tell you things you never listened. You just said I'd grow out of it or something. Oh, I know maybe I didn't want to marry her—not so soon, anyway. But now I am married to her. And—look—I'm not going to be shoved around, see—any more! And we're going to have that baby—and keep it—and stay married—and—"

"What about college? What about that?"

"I don't care about college. I don't care. If they take me back, they'll take me back as a married man, with a baby. Do you understand? If they won't take me back that way, they won't take me back at all."

There was only the briefest pause; then his mother said, "Who do you think will pay your bills, my dear? Not Daddy. You can be sure of that."

"All right; if he won't then I won't go back to college at all."

"How will you earn a living? How will you get a job?"

"I'll—I'll drive a truck!"

A tremor came into her voice now. "Teddy, you're insane. You're absolutely insane. Haven't you brought enough disgrace on us? Don't you see—"

"Quiet. Just be quiet. You see—there's one thing you don't seem to get, Mother, and that's that I'm in love wih Carol. Do you hear? Oh, I know I was scared at first, when I found out. Who wouldn't be? We made a mistake. So we're going to pay for it. But the right way. Not your way. *The right way!*"

The silence now on the other end of the wire was longer. Then his mother said in an even voice, "What if we cut off the money right now? Right this minute?"

"Go ahead!"

"I'm going to put your father back on the wire!"

"No, you're not," he said, "because this time I will hang up. You see? I'm going to hang up. Good-bye." He held the receiver for a moment in his hand, then replaced it on the hook. Not with a slam, but squarely.

He stood there, looking at it, half expecting something to happen, for it to come alive. Then he picked up his cigarette from the edge of the night stand, put it to his lips, inhaled, and blew out a sharp stream of smoke. He stared at the telephone a few moments longer. His expression changed rapidly, running the gamut from anger to something akin to fear, to triumph. Although his twentieth birthday was still two months off, he looked, for these moments, both older and younger. He turned on his heel. "Carol!" he called, and strode toward the door. "Carol!"

She still sat on the chaise, on the now-quite-dark terrace. As he stepped out and walked toward her, she looked up at him. On the chaise in front of her he saw a pale sheaf of papers, stapled together.

"I signed the adoption papers," she said simply.

He sat down beside her.

"I signed them," she said. "Not because of what your parents said. But I sat here thinking and I thought, what business do we have bringing a child into the world? You and I? Two weaklings . . ."

He lifted the sheaf of papers from the chaise; she seemed suddenly to guess his intent and tried to grab them back. For a brief moment they struggled. "We don't always have to be weaklings, do we?" he asked. "Do we? Do we?" Then as he began to tear them, bits of paper flew about the terrace in the breeze. They clung to each other. Suddenly they both began to laugh, even though they were both already crying.

"DO YOU BELIEVE IN CHANGE?"

✿✿✿✿ It was a Sunday afternoon late in August. The California sun had been blazing with such fierceness all day that the temperature there in the Central Valley had been well over a hundred since noon—the same still, dry heat that characterized Valley weather from June to October. As the two of them sat in the parked car, tall young men in dungarees walked by with lazy strides, turning now and then to watch the girls in the park, who wandered carelessly in damp cotton dresses, scuffing the sand under the swings by the tennis courts. As a convertible passed slowly, the boys turned and the girls in the car gave them provocative looks; then the car speeded up and turned the corner. The pace of the day had slowed, too, to a tempo of carelessness and ease as the sun stretched long, reflective fingers through the shroud of leaves that hung over the street. A leaf fell and caught in the vent of his car. The first leaf of autumn, Mark thought.

"Do you have to use that?" she asked. "Do you have to use that cigarette holder?"

He held it self-consciously. "I quit smoking for a long time," he explained. "Then I started up again two or three weeks ago."

She didn't answer him or seem interested any more. Instead, she put her arm on the frame of the car window and looked across the park. The tennis balls fell from the rackets with a slow *pop . . . pop.* "It's getting late," she said.

He watched her—her slim, tanned legs below her white shorts, her bare feet placed firmly on the floor of the car. "I had forgotten how short you are," he said.

"I've done my hair differently," she said.

"I like it," he said. "It's very attractive."

"It's very short."

The leaf trapped in the open vent fluttered, then another leaf fell and rested for a moment on the hood. "I'd like to make these Sunday visits a regular thing," he said softly. "That is, if you have no objection."

She seemed to think about this. "I have no objection," she said finally. "Only I—let's see—I may be busy on *some* Sundays."

"That's all right," he said. "I don't mean that it has to be like clockwork, like a rigid schedule or anything. Just on Sundays when it's convenient for you."

"I'd like to have some notice of when you're coming," she said, "some notice in advance."

"That's why I thought we could make it more or less a standing date," he said. "So there won't be a lot of bother and fuss ahead of time. You could drop me a line. . . ."

"I'm a little confused," she said. "I don't really understand why these visits should begin now. After all, it's been over a year. Billy is nearly six months old, and you evidently haven't felt it was necessary to pay a visit before this. And theoretically, I suppose, you could have."

"I've been down before," he said. "You know that."

"Once," she said, "when it was hardly convenient."

"Is that the only time you know about?"

"I know about the time when I was in the hospital, trying to hang on to the baby, and you came at ten o'clock at night and woke up my mother and created a scene on our front steps."

He knew he had to watch his words carefully. "Actually," he said, "I came down here four other times. Didn't they tell you?"

"No."

"The last time was very pleasant. William called the police to order me off the property."

"William is my brother-in-law," she said. "He had my best interests at heart."

He thought to himself, We must not quarrel. "Look," he said, "I could just telephone you, couldn't I, ahead of time to see whether or not you're busy?"

"Well," she said, "I really think I'd better go over it with Mr. Gurney and get his opinion."

He had placed himself on fragile ground, he realized. So he decided to let it drop there, not to press it any further. "Very well," he said. "Whatever you think."

"Do you want to go inside now?" she asked.

"All right."

They got out of the car and he followed her up the walk to the house. The pavement was still hot and she walked gingerly on her bare feet.

In the living room, while he waited for her, the maid appeared.

"Hello, Doris," he said. "I've got thousands—literally thousands—of green trading stamps for you. I've been saving them for you for over a year—every time I buy gas. When I bought my car I paid cash for it and asked for the green stamps, but it seems that that's against the rules. I don't want them myself. I'll bring them down the next time I come."

Presently Helen came down the stairs carrying the baby.

For a long while they sat on the floor with Billy between them. He talked to the baby in a soft voice, and Helen sat cross-legged, saying nothing. "Do you like it here?" he asked. "Do you like it here in this pretty house? Do they feed you enough? I don't think they feed you enough—tell Mommy that you're nothing but a bag of bones, just a bag of bones." To let Helen know that he wasn't serious he laughed as he said these things.

"Where did he get the little red suit?" he asked her.

"It was a present," she said. "Someone gave it to him."

"Who?"

"I don't remember."

"Well, it's very handsome," he said. "Yes, it's very handsome. And look how handsome he is—much handsomer than even his mommy or his daddy. Who does he look like?"

"Everyone has a different opinion," she said.

"I think he looks like my father," Mark said. "I don't think he looks like either of us."

The baby started crawling slowly across the floor toward him.

"I think he knows me," he said. "I think he knows who I am. I think he knows by instinct. Do you believe in instinct?"

"I don't know," she said.

"I do. I think we know our fathers and mothers by instinct. Does he act this friendly with everyone?"

"I'm afraid so," she said.

"Well, I'm glad to hear that, anyway," he said.

"He's really very good."

"Isn't he large? How much did he weigh when he was born?"

'Seven thirteen."

"Is that average?"

"Fairly, yes."

"May I pick him up?"

"Yes, but don't get your face close to him if you have a cold."

"I'm just getting over one," he said. He picked the baby up and held him on his knee. "Pat-a-cake, pat-a-cake, baker's man, bake me a cake as fast as you can. . . . I've forgotten the rest."

"So have I."

"We must look that one up."

The room grew dark, and looking up from the baby now and then, he watched Helen as she sat with her face averted, turned to the shadows. He thought that her features had attained a sharpness, an angularity. There was something in her face that he couldn't recognize. Wondering whether it was time or pain or suffering, he asked, "Is he much trouble?"

"All babies are trouble."

"Night feedings—that sort of thing?"

"Not any more."

Doris came through the room with a tray of drinks. "Your mother wants to know if you'd like one," she said to Helen.

"No, thank you, Doris."

Doris went through the living room and out to the terrace. Outside, voices rose and fell in conversation. Some of the voices Mark recognized. "When are you going to Bermuda, Mrs. W?" William was asking.

"Oh, never, never, never! Or so it seems with all the work I have to do," Mrs. Warren answered.

Ice tinkled in the glasses on the terrace.

"I suppose you want one," Helen said.

"What?"

"A drink. Do you? I suppose I could get you one."

"No, thank you," he said.

Nothing has changed, he thought. The smell of Scotch whiskey on a Sunday afternoon on the terrace, the sound of drinks being mixed, new bottles opened, case after case of Scotch for week after week of Mrs. Warren's entertaining. There was a new voice outside now.

"Arlene, what's happened?" a woman's voice said.

"Nothing, dear. Come on in. Mark is here to see the baby."

"Oh! I'll come back later. Fred and I thought we could buy you a drink."

"No, *no!* Sit down. We're having drinks out here. They're in the living room. Please, I want you both to stay."

"I don't drink any more," Mark said to Helen.

"Is that so?"

"Yes. It was one of the things that ruined us, wasn't it? My drinking."

"It was *the* thing," Helen said.

"Yes. So I stopped altogether. It wasn't easy."

"No, I imagine it wasn't," she said. "Are you an Alcoholics Anonymous or something?"

"No, this was a thing that I did all by myself."

"It was always so funny with you," she said. "I never could understand. After all, all of us here in town—we've always managed to drink. But somehow we always managed to *maintain.* You never could. With you, it was always ugly."

"Yes, I know. I don't make any excuses for myself. That's why," he said, "I thought possibly we might try again."

She looked at him now. It was as though for the first time since he'd arrived she was genuinely interested in what he was

saying. "Look," she said, "we're not children any more. There's
no point in fooling ourselves, is there? You can't just ask me to
forget—like that—ever. What about the thing with the bureau
drawer? What about the time you cut my hair? What about the
night that fellow came home with you—and I—" her voice almost broke—"and I was there waiting? And you said all those
terrible things. And the night Father died and you were nowhere to be found. Oh, you were *there*—sometimes—but never
really there. I needed you then, Mark."

"I know, I know," he said. He thought, I must be careful,
careful. We must not quarrel. He turned to the baby.

"And when the princess awoke the next morning, she found
that her frog had turned into a handsome prince," he said.

"What are you talking about?" Helen asked.

"I'm trying to remember some of the stories."

"What stories?"

"The stories I used to be told when I was little."

He held the baby's head between his hands. "I'm glad I met
you," he whispered. "I'm glad I came. Do you realize it took a
lot of courage to come down here? Do you know that?"

"A lot of what?" she asked.

"Courage."

For hours before, he had driven around the town, noticing
changes, noticing the things he remembered. He had driven past
the Warrens' house three or four times, afraid to stop, and then
he had stopped driving around it, afraid that someone in the
house would notice him. Then he had left the car on the other
side of the park and got out and walked through it, watching
the tennis players, not daring to look across to the white house
that showed through the trees. He found three comic books on
a park bench and sat down to read them. Mothers with their

children wandered in the park, and from time to time he would look up to see if by some chance . . . Then he had left the park and walked down the street, knowing what he must do and thinking, No, no, I can't . . . I haven't the courage. I can't go there, ever. . . . And then asking himself the question: What do you want from them? Do you want the police again and the bitterness and the locked doors and drawn curtains and the voice from the upstairs window: "Go away. We have all decided . . ."

Then in the ease and shadows as the day darkened he had felt better, and he walked back to his car and drove it to the house, got out, and walked up to the front door. Mrs. Warren had answered the door herself.

"Is this what they told you you could do?" she asked him.

"No, but I'd like very much to see the baby," he said. "If that's possible and you don't mind."

She had seemed undecided. "Well, I think he's asleep right now," she said.

"Then later, perhaps?"

"Well—well, come in, Mark. Come in and sit down. I'll tell Helen you're here."

Their baby sat on his knee now and Helen said, "You'd better give him back to me. It's almost time for his supper." He rose and handed her the baby.

"My darling," she said. "My own darling little boy!"

"Helen . . ." he began.

"Yes?"

"Helen, if you're going to feed him, could I watch?"

"It's not very interesting to watch him have his dinner, actually," she said. "He spits up everything sometimes. He—"

"I don't want to interfere with any schedule."

"Perhaps some other time, Mark. I think he's had enough excitement for one day."

"Yes, yes, I agree."

Only hold out a little longer, he thought. Only one, two minutes more. "Next time I come . . ." he began.

"When will that be, Mark?"

"Next Sunday?"

"Very well. Only I think—no, I don't think so. No, I really don't think you can. I think you'd really better work through Mr. Gurney, and perhaps after I have my decree—"

"I don't want a divorce."

"Well, I'm afraid there's very little you can do about it."

He started to say something abrupt again, but he checked himself. "All right," he said. "I'll work through Mr. Gurney."

As they talked she was slowly but surely walking him toward the door.

"Let me hold him once more," he said. He took him and then blurted it out—not only to her but also to the child in his arms—in the form of a question that his child could not at this time answer and which required no answer from anyone else. It was an assertion, too, of what he believed his own rights in the matter to be. "When you're older," he said, "you and I will spend a great deal of time together. We'll take trips and go hunting together, and you'll spend at least half your life with me—because you're half mine, anyway."

"If you have a cold," Helen said, "I'd rather you didn't hold your face so close. Here, let me have him."

Suddenly, as the baby was lifted from his arms to hers, he began to cry, and Mark, taking him back almost roughly, held on to his son desperately, urgently. "Oh, it's a bum life," he said. "Isn't it? Isn't it a bum life? What's to become of you?"

"He'll be all right," Helen said.

"Do you believe in change?" he asked her. "Do you believe that people have the ability to change? That's what it all hangs upon, isn't it—whether you do or do not believe that in over a year I might have changed?"

"I don't believe in fairy tales," she said. "Frogs turning into princes . . ."

"I'm talking about the future. I don't give a damn about the past. But this is the future, right here."

"Your cold, Mark," she said, and firmly took the baby away from him.

She opened the door and he stepped outside. The baby was quiet in her arms, and knowing that the moment, the visit, was nearly over, Mark turned and went halfway down the steps.

An orange giant of a moon topped the trees and on everything was a pale light in a haze of fog that floated in from the riverbanks. In the pools of moonlight on the street a boy went by on a bicycle. Suddenly Mark saw that she had followed him and was standing close behind him with the baby in her arms.

"I believe, I believe," she whispered. Helen took a step backward from him and held out her free hand.

"Next Sunday is all right," she said. "Just come, I mean. You don't have to call Mr. Gurney."

He felt he had to tell her now or he never would. "Helen," he said, "look—it isn't just Billy that I want to see. Can you imagine why I really came?"

"Yes."

"Billy was only a toe hold—a way to get my foot in the door. I wanted to see you, Helen."

In the dark she turned to him intensely. Her voice was soft, urgent. "Meet me somewhere," she said. "Somewhere where we can just talk and be alone. Because I want you too, Mark. I always have—I've always known—but there were always so many others, so many people who intruded, who had their own ideas, and who started telling me what to do: Mother, William, Mr. Gurney. Did they ever think that this was a problem just for the two of us, the three? Did they?" Her voice broke. "I mean, we *do* have things to say to each other and we do have to be alone, don't we?"

"Then you do believe," he said.

"Yes. Let's make a date. You can pick me up somewhere, anywhere you say, and we'll go somewhere and just talk and be alone."

"Oh, my darling," he said.

She began to laugh now, almost hysterically. "Write to me and disguise your writing. Oh, darling, isn't this like a B movie? Oh, darling, isn't it? But it will have a happy ending, won't it? Don't B movies always have happy endings?"

"Yes," he said. "Yes, yes."

He knew he must leave her now or burst with happiness. "I'll write to you," he said.

Behind them, the door of the house opened. "Helen, dear," Mrs. Warren called, "Auntie Alice is on the phone from Santa Monica."

Helen pulled her hand away from his. "Good night," she whispered.

Mark unlocked his car and got inside. "I don't believe in miracles overnight," he said aloud to no one. "No, I don't believe in miracles overnight, but perhaps in time—" He had to wait a moment before driving away until the tears that filled his eyes went away—tears of happiness and misery. He wanted to feel this new thing, this queer promise, and suddenly the weeks and months ahead seemed longer and harder than any of the whispering, churning months behind.

BETWEEN THE MAPLES

✿✿✿✿ Mr. Fiedler sat on his piazza in a pair of heavy brown slacks and red canvas sandals with cork soles, and drank a Scotch-and-soda as the sun went down. He looked out across the parched lawn that had been burned to a crisp brown by the summer drought and the sea air, and waited for Dolores. It was hard to tell just when Dolores would appear, or from where—whether it would be from the path through the thick hedge along the lane, or up the gravel driveway and through the house, or through the oak grove and across the back lawn— carrying her riding boots in her hand, if it was especially warm, and walking barefoot, or in slippers, swinging her crop in her hand. But when Dolores came she would say something like, "I saw you sitting here, between the maples," and Mr. Fiedler would say, "They're red oaks, not maples, dear," and she would laugh. And then there would be such a silence, such a hush, and under the lantern light, or in the sun, if any sun remained— whichever it happened to be—Mr. Fiedler would look at Dolores' slim legs and small breasts, the legs so much slimmer in her whipcord jodhpurs, the breasts so much smaller under the flannel shirt she sometimes wore, and smile.

"Bring out the portable radio, Martha, please," Mr. Fiedler said when the maid appeared at the door. "I want to get the six-o'clock news."

Martha pouted. "I'm busy," she said. "You could get it yourself if you'd walk two steps."

Mr. Fiedler was very cool. "What are you here for, Martha?" he asked. And he added, "Let's not have any temper tonight, lamb chop."

"Lamb chop yourself!" Martha said.

"Martha?" he said sweetly. "Has anyone ever told you that you have the disposition of a steel file?" And then, as an added touch of malice, he said, "And has it ever been suggested that you might retire from your profession? You may be getting a bit old to be the perfect house servant."

Martha gave him a long, straight look, "D'you think maybe that was why I was hired?" she asked him. She turned and went into the house.

Mr. Fiedler was a tall, thin man with a longish face and close-cropped gray hair that was stiff and yellowed from the sun, and a small—very small and carefully clipped—mustache. His tan, which he had worked so industriously on all summer, had begun to fade and, in the mirror that morning as he shaved, he had wondered if his still-handsome face was beginning to look a little pale. (His increasing pallor was one of the things he dreaded most about the winters here.) Reaching now, with his fingers, he tried to rub color into his thin cheeks. The thumb and forefinger of his right hand were bandaged with fresh adhesive tape from where, this afternoon, he had hammered himself trying, without success, to repair his collapsing dock.

As he sat, to the east of him he could see the black rockiness of the Maine seacoast, shiny as a lizard's back, and the beach, which was nothing but a bank of small quartz pebbles and shattered conch shells; and behind him, his house with its broad, scattered-stone terrace and the row of butter tubs, painted spanking white, filled with house azalea and geraniums and blue lobelia. In the distance now, Mr. Fiedler could hear the sound of footsteps on the driveway, that peculiarly summery sound of feet on loose gravel. Dolores? In the silence that followed he could almost hear the buzzing of the big cow flies as they struck against the wire mesh of the screen door. (And *Phyllophaga,* he thought with a little shudder—June beetles— and the insects he hated most—batting against the bulb of the porch light, and falling scorched and smashed on the steps, their great, milky bodies . . .) Shifting uneasily in his chair and tapping his foot impatiently on the stone, he wrenched his thoughts back to the person whose footsteps might now be moving quickly toward him.

"Hello, there!"

Mr. Fiedler shaded his eyes. Dolores was standing in the yard. "Never mind the radio, Martha!" Mr. Fiedler shouted. "I have a caller."

Just as always before, Dolores had her jodhpurs on. She was in stocking feet, carrying her boots and her hat in her hands. She pushed a damp lock of hair from her face and began talking rapidly. "I saw you through the maples!" she said.

"Oh, God!" said Mr. Fiedler, laughing. "They're red oaks, not maples, my love!"

She smiled at him. *"Quercus borealis,"* she said. "See? I was teasing you. Do I get an A?"

Dolores dropped her boots on the stone. "I've never been so exhausted in my life! Freddie had me doing jumps till my fanny was black and blue. Then Saucer took the bit and gave me a terrific spin! I can't tell you how scared I was. I pulled and pulled and Saucer kept right on *galloping!*" She laughed. "It wasn't hard for Freddie to see that I'm still no good with horses."

Mr. Fiedler laughed. "Sit down, dear." He motioned to one of the metal chairs.

"Oh, your *fingers!* What happened to them?"

He wagged the bandaged fingers at her. "Bashed them with a hammer, trying to fix the dock," he said. "I'm going to have to call a man to do it. I've decided that I may be an artisan with life but not with a carpenter's tools."

"Just like me," she said. "I'm no good at *any*thing."

"How many times have I told you not to underrate yourself? Can I get you a drink?"

"Oh, no, thanks," said Dolores. "You should know the answer to *that* question by now."

"Not even a Coke?"

"No, thanks. Whew!" Dolores sat down and stretched her stockinged feet into a patch of remaining sunlight. "My socks are full of holes. Look at them. Mother says I wear out a dozen pairs of socks a week. I'm going to have to order a gross of them before I go back to college." Bending down, she began to pull off the socks.

Mr. Fiedler took another sip from his glass. "I'm glad you dropped in," he said. "I was just beginning to get lonely."

"Oh, you've been so nice to let me come!" Dolores said. There was a small embarrassed silence, and she laughed nervously. "I feel I've almost made this my second home. I'm awfully grateful."

Mr. Fiedler looked at her intently. "When are you going back?"

"The fifteenth." She looked at the ground. "So this is—sort of to say good-by. And thank you for everything."

"But the fifteenth is a week away!"

"I know, but—well, I have to pack and everything."

"I'll miss you."

"That's sweet of you. I'll always think of—well, of this, when I think of Maine."

"You can't get used to it, can you?"

"Maine? Oh, yes. At least I'm beginning to. But after all—it's such a *little* town, this place. Five hundred people! I mean, there just can't be more than one or two *intelligent* people in a town of only five hundred people. Let's see," she said, counting the people off on her fingertips, "in addition to Mother and Father—who probably shouldn't count anyway—there's just been you and Freddy. That's all."

"Sometimes one or two are enough."

"Oh, don't get me wrong—I'm beginning to love it. I'm beginning to love the *hack*matacks, and the *tam*aracks, and I can tell poison ivy from arbutus and woodbine from coreopsis! I've learned so much this summer. You've taught me so much . . ."

"Botany is just a hobby with me, pet," Mr. Fiedler said with a little smile. "I'm afraid I've bored you with it."

"Bored? Do you think I'd have kept dropping over and dropping over if I'd been bored? I've been fascinated—ever since I first came short-cutting home through your oak grove and said, 'What pretty maple trees!' "

"I thought you were a dryad," he said. "I could give you a course in Maine wildlife, too. Which reminds me, we've never had our bird walk."

"Oh, I *know.* I'm sorry. Next summer, maybe." She was holding the white socks in a little ball in her hand. Reaching down, she stuffed the ball inside one of the boots. "You've opened whole new horizons for me this summer," she said. "You really have."

"I'd like to teach you more." Mr. Fiedler said. He leaned forward in his chair. "Poetry, for instance." Smiling at her, he said in a soft voice:

"Ce n'est plus une ardeur dans mes veines cachée:
C'est Vénus toute entière à sa proie attachée . . ."

"What is that?" she asked him.

"Racine."

"Freddie writes poetry, did you know that? He writes sonnets. He told me that today."

Mr. Fiedler stirred in his chair and crossed his long legs. He looked down at Dolores' bare feet. Her toenails were lacquered a pale pink. "Love in bloom," he said.

"Oh, nonsense!"

"He's very handsome."

"Do you think so?"

"Yes." Mr. Fiedler looked up and studied carefully the expression on the girl's face. There were delicate lines he noticed, particularly about the mouth and eyes, squint lines from the sun like fine wrinkles in brown tissue paper. "I'm having a cold lobster tonight," he said. "Would you join me for supper?"

"No, I couldn't. Mother expects me back for dinner at seven."

"I'm not going to accept that excuse much longer."

"I'm afraid you'll have to while Mother's Mother. Thanks, anyway."

Martha came to the door. "Do you want anything for the young lady?" she asked.

"Please just have a Coke," said Mr. Fiedler. "It would make me feel so much better."

"All right."

"And another Scotch for me, Martha."

"Yes, sir."

When Martha had gone back into the house, Mr. Fiedler crinkled his nose confidentially and said, "Do you think she's a spy? Do you think she's spying on me? She's always poking about and sticking her nose in on me whenever I have a caller. I think Louise—"

"Hush, hush," said Dolores. "I'm sure she wouldn't do a thing like that."

"Oh, wouldn't she? You don't know Louise."

"I'm sorry," Dolores said. There was a silence, and then she said, "How is Mrs. Fiedler?"

He waved his hand. "Same as ever, I'm afraid. She's off seeing her doctor, as usual."

"Poor thing."

"Her troubles are purely psychogenic, pet, as I've explained to you."

"I know. But I like her. She looks . . . very sweet."

He raised his eyebrows. "Oh? You've met Louise?"

"Not really. But I saw her the other day, in the grocery store. I was buying some cheese-and-olive spread for Mother, and I saw her—I heard her give her name, you know. For the charge account."

"I see."

"I thought she had a very sweet face. A very dear face."

"Sweet with suffering, you mean?" he asked her.

"No, not that. Not really. A brave face, I guess I mean."

Dolores raised herself in her chair and tucked her feet underneath her. With one hand, she rubbed her forearm. "I think I got some of that stuff today," she said. "You know, poison oak or poison ivy."

"Let me see." Mr. Fiedler got up from his chair and crossed the terrace to where Dolores sat. He took her hand and examined the arm closely, pulling up the sleeve of the green jacket. "It looks like a good case of nettles," he said. "Let me get you some witch hazel."

"Oh, don't bother, please. It'll go away in a minute, I'm sure."

"No bother at all." Mr. Fiedler walked over to the door and into the house. Dolores stood up and went slowly to the edge of the terrace and looked out at the sea beyond the rocks and the juniper bushes, at the whitecaps breaking far out in the slanting sun and the tide sweeping in toward the land. She yawned and stretched herself, and unbuttoned the green riding jacket and slipped it off. Then she tucked the tails of her white blouse in around the waistband of her jodhpurs. She went back to her chair, sat down, and put one foot across one knee. Critically she examined the bare foot, rubbing the sole with her fingertips and brushing the sand from between her toes. "Whose are these huaraches?" she said when Mr. Fiedler came back out with the bottle of witch hazel in his hand.

"Louise's."

"May I borrow them? When the sun gets off this terrace, these stones are *cold.*"

"Sure." Mr. Fiedler picked them up from where they lay under a chair. "Here you are. Probably acres too big for you." He handed them to Dolores. "Oh-oh, I forgot something. Have you got a Kleenex I can use as a swab?"

"No," Dolores said. "But I'm brave. Just put it on straight."

Mr. Fiedler emptied some of the clear liquid into his cupped palm and rubbed it gently, in smooth, bladelike strokes, up and down Dolores' arm. "Feel better?" he asked.

Martha, just then, coming out with two glasses in her hands, said, "Here's your Scotch. And here's your Coke, miss."

"I'm sure we wouldn't be able to tell the difference if you didn't point it out to us, Martha," said Mr. Fiedler.

And then, when Martha had left, he said, "Here's a toast to the summer crowd. I couldn't live without 'em." He drank deeply.

Dolores sat, half turned in her chair, looking at the ocean. "It's such a beautiful view from here," she said.

"I'm like Gertrude Stein," Mr. Fiedler said. "I like a view, but I like to sit with my back to it."

"You're the best-read person I've ever met," she said. Suddenly she clapped a hand over her mouth. "Oh! I forgot to bring back your *book!*"

"Did you read it?"

"Well, *most* of it. I thought it was—very interesting."

"You may not be ready for Baudelaire," he said with a little smile. "I have another book for you—a very special book that I picked out for you in my library this morning."

"But how would I get it back to you? Well, I could mail it, I guess."

Mr. Fiedler hitched his chair over closer to her. "If you promise to come back next summer, I may let you keep it," he said.

About half an hour later Dolores was saying, "Freddie's different because he's funny. He's the only boy I've met who could say funny things, things that I really wanted to laugh at, and he's the only person that I've met who hasn't wanted to take me seriously."

"Including me?" said Mr. Fiedler.

Dolores looked up from where she lay, on her stomach on the terrace with her chin in her hands, her half-filled glass in front of her. "Of course not including you," she said. "You're different, too. You're a friend, and—well, a special kind of friend."

He leaned toward her, his glass pressed between his hands. "Special? In what way?"

"Well . . ." She drew a vague pattern on the stone with her index finger. "I don't know." She paused. "I guess it's because you treat me like an equal. Like an adult. My parents have never *thought* of treating me like an adult. Why, you even offer me a drink—even though I don't drink! And you offer me cigarettes. And besides, you're very interesting to talk to."

"Perhaps I see the woman you're capable of being."

"Yes. But you know, it's funny," she said. "And I don't mean *funny*. But I wonder."

"What do you wonder?"

"Well, it seems so *unusual* that a person like you—a great intellectual, really—should have given up jobs at some of the most famous girls' schools in the country, even Burneyside— and come way up here to Maine to live, to this dinky town, miles from everywhere, and live year round. . . ."

"What do you know about Burneyside?" he said.

"Nothing—except that you taught there, didn't you? And—"

"Next thing," he said, raising his glass to his lips, "you're going to tell me you suspect I was dismissed from my job at Burneyside."

"No, I don't mean that," she said. "But—well, it does seem strange."

"I pursue my researches up here," he said a little crossly. "In peace."

"I know, I know. But don't you ever miss—"

"Never," he said. He took a swallow of his drink.

"Do you know something?" he said quickly. "A little bird has just whispered something in my ear. A little bird tells me that somebody has been talking to you about me, somebody in town, saying such things as—"

"Oh, don't be silly! I just meant—"

"Saying that I live off a rich, sick wife? Hmm? Things like that? Am I right? Did my little bird tell me true, because this little town is notorious, my pet, for—"

"No, no. I've never talked to *anybody* about you, except—"

"Aha!" he said, leaning forward again. "Except whom?"

"Well, except Freddie, of course."

"I see."

"But Freddie's never said anything about *you*. You see, I think Freddie's a rather special kind of person, too. I think you'd like him if you got to know him. He's very witty. Do you know he's the only person who can keep me laughing all the time? Not just because he says funny things, but the way he says them, you know, that's so funny?" She put it as a question and then laughed. "I guess I don't know what I mean," she said, "but you understand. I like to talk things over with you. Today, when we were riding, he just suddenly reached over and grabbed my hand and said, 'A person doesn't need to have a memory to remember what you look like.' I'd told him I was leaving on the fifteenth, you see. But wasn't that—I mean, wasn't that a sweet thing to say? And I didn't know what to answer, so I just laughed. And then *he* started laughing, and I was honestly afraid I was going to laugh myself sick, I laughed so hard. And do you know what he said New York is? He said New York is a place where the farmers are Democrats instead of Republicans. I asked him if he'd ever been to New York, and that's what he said. Don't you think that's funny?"

"Ha-ha," said Mr. Fiedler.

"And it's like that with everything—everything he says. Why, the other day—"

"He's never said anything about me?"

"Of course not," she said. "Why should he?"

"And your mother—or father?"

"I don't have to discuss *every*thing with my parents, do I?" she said.

Mr. Fiedler chuckled softly. "In addition to its charming flora and fauna, this village is noted for its malicious gossips," he said. "They delight in spreading ugly stories about anyone who—how shall I say—who seems to be a bit different, or perhaps better, than they are."

"Oh, I'm sure they do!" Dolores said.

"If what's-his-name—your young Freddie—ever did say anything . . . or if anyone else did . . . you wouldn't believe it, would you? Any more than you'd believe that patently obvious line he's handing you?"

"It isn't a line. It's—"

"How can you tell? How old are you? Seventeen?" Mr. Fiedler's voice was very hard. "Give yourself a few more years to find out, pet."

Dolores looked at her fingernails. "Please don't be cross with me for telling you. I—"

"That's okay." Mr. Fiedler stood up abruptly. "It just makes me sad—literally ill—to hear you talking the way you've been about this—this red-necked young riding instructor. You don't know what love is."

Dolores made a steeple of her fingers and rested her chin on their tips, flattening her elbows against the stones, and as she did so her white blouse came untucked around her waist.

"You see?" he said, standing above her. "You yawn, you stretch, you laugh, your blouse comes prettily out of your jodhpurtops. You're young, you see, and—"

"Huh?" Dolores laughed and reached around to tuck in her blouse.

"Dolores," said Mr. Fiedler. He knelt on the terrace beside her.

"What?" Dolores laughed again, but this time the laugh was briefer. "You're a funny person," she said. "You say the strangest things . . ."

"Can you keep a secret?"

She sat up abruptly. "No."

"Why not, Dolores?"

"Because I don't want to. I'll betray it if you tell me, so please don't."

"But I want to."

"No, no . . ."

Mr. Fiedler stood up once more. "Let me have that glass," he said. As he reached for it, his hand trembled. "I mean just don't say you're in love with him. How's the arm?"

Dolores showed it to him. "I think it's gone away. What time is it?"

"Nearly seven."

"I've got to go."

"Please stay," he said tensely.

"I really must—"

"You're just a little dear in those jodhpurs, Dolores."

"Am I?"

"Yes. A little beauty. Here, let—"

Dolores jumped to her feet. "You should save those things for your wife," she said. She picked up the green jacket.

"You don't know what it's like, Dolores, living with a woman like that."

Dolores shivered. "Why do you—" she began.

Mr. Fiedler seized the girl's shoulders, and turned her around to face him. "Why do *you?* Why do you behave so foolishly? Don't you know that *I'm* not poison? Do you want a cigarette?" He fumbled in his slacks pocket for a pack.

"No, thanks. I must—"

He still gripped her shoulders. " 'The poet—' " he said in a hollow voice " '—the poet is like a prince of the clouds, who haunts the tempest and laughs at the archer—exiled to the noisy earth, his giant's wings—' " He dropped his hands suddenly, and his voice caught as if he were choking. And he turned his head sharply away from her. When he spoke again his voice was a whisper. " 'Whose giant's wings keep him from walking,' " he finished. "Baudelaire. That was Baudelaire. Do you ever see what I'm talking about, Dolores?"

"I don't think so."

Once more he reached for her arm, but this time she stepped away from him. "Wait a minute," he said. "Please. Look. Oh, God, I'm sorry if I—but listen," he said, "just listen a minute, can't you? Do you want to know what it's like? You asked me, didn't you, how I endured this place? Do you want to know? Do you want to know what it's like to be a man who never, not once in his life, has ever achieved a single thing he's wanted?

Do you? Even at Burneyside, when they said I— *Wait!*" he said, as she took another step away from him.

Across the terrace someone called, "Dolores!"

"It's Freddie," Dolores said. "He wants to walk me home. I have to go."

She pushed her arms into the sleeves of her jacket. "Thanks for the huaraches," she said, kicking them off. "I'll walk home barefoot. Coming, Freddie!" she called.

"Wait a minute—I'll get that book."

"I'll—I'll pick it up some other time."

"Wait. You'll catch your death walking that way. Tell him to—"

Dolores laughed nervously. "Please," she said. "I'm sorry. Please tell Mrs. Fiedler good-by for me, and—"

"That boy isn't worth it."

"Tell her I'm—"

"She knows. She's upstairs."

"Upstairs? But I thought—"

"She's upstairs whenever I'm downstairs. Do you see what I mean?"

"Yes. Well—good-by. Thank you so much for—"

"Tomorrow?"

"Yes. That is, I will if Freddie—" She broke off. "I hope so, really. Well, good-by, and—"

Mr. Fiedler tried to take her hand. "Good night," she said. She picked up her gloves and riding crop from the terrace and, taking a boot in each hand, ran barefoot across the stones and across the lawn toward the trees.

When she met Freddie, Dolores said, "Let's run!" And they started running along the ocean's edge, flat-footed, across the rocks and stretches of pebbly beach, between the clumps of sand grass and juniper. Just before they reached the cottage, she stopped suddenly.

"Wait!" she said. "Wait till I get my breath." She knew there were tears in her eyes. "I don't think I like him now, really. In fact," she said, "I was kind of scared. It was funny, Freddie . . . he was so queer tonight. . . . I—I feel so odd, scared and excited, as though I've avoided something, or outgrown something. Do you see . . . ?"

"Sure," he said. "I see."

"You're so wonderful, Freddie!" Quite impulsively, she clutched his arm and pressed her fingers into his sunburned flesh to feel the heat and the muscle and the strength of it. "You *do* understand! Oh, Freddie, do I look older? Do I look like a woman at last? Do I?"

After watching Dolores, Mr. Fiedler went into the house, down the steps into the pine-paneled living room, holding his cigarette, unlighted, looking for a match. Martha was across the hall, in the dining room, setting the table. "Martha?" he called. "Where are the matches?"

"I'm sure I wouldn't know," Martha said.

Mr. Fiedler raised his voice. "I said where are they! Please get them for me immediately! I want a match for my cigarette! Didn't I tell you to put matches in all the bowls?"

"That's not my job," said Martha. "I've got other things to keep me busy, thank you."

Mr. Fiedler rushed into the dining room. Martha was putting silver on the table, and the silver candlesticks on either side of the centerpiece were moist and perspiring in the warm air. "How dare you?" he screamed. "How dare you to speak to me like that? Get out! Get out of this house!"

"I take my orders from Mrs. Fiedler, sir."

Mr. Fiedler ran back into the hall and halfway up the stairs. "Louise!" he screamed from the landing, his voice becoming higher and shriller and harsher with every syllable. "Get that woman out of here before I kill her! Louise!" And when she didn't answer, he cried, "Don't worry! It's safe! Everybody's gone, nothing's happened, it's safe! You can come down now!"

The Partly Joined

THE BACKGAMMON TABLE

✿✿✿✿ It was made of pink marble. Irene Silton called the color antique pigeon's blood and was convinced, from some hieroglyphics scratched on the underside of the stone, that it was very old—at least a hundred and fifty years old, she thought—and had been quarried in Algeria. Standing where it did, on a slim wrought-iron pedestal in their living room, it seemed to drink in the winter sunlight from Seventieth Street, and to reflect this light back from some interior place. The stone's veins and clouds seemed deeper than the polished surface, as though a whole landscape of ridges and arroyos lay crystallized and buried there beneath a flat and glassy layer. Often, when she was alone in the house, Irene would go to the table and stand gazing into this wild and sunlit country, her fingertips resting on the table's cool, smooth edge, dreaming of what it must be like to live among such frozen mountains and caverns.

Justin and Irene had been taking a walk when Irene had spotted the table, covered with dust and clutter, in the window of a shop on Lexington Avenue. It was an odd little shop, full of what nots and gimcrackery, full of lamps with beaded shades, pockmarked pewterware, crazed Staffordshire plates, and bronze

statues of fat and leering cherubs—a confused and totally un-
memorable little shop. In fact, it was quite surprising that she
had even looked in the window; it was not the sort of shop
that usually interested her. But she had looked in—her eye
drawn to it by something—and there, with its pedestal base
wrapped in yellowed newspaper and tied with cord, its top piled
high with empty picture frames, it was.

"Justin!" she had said, seizing his arm. "Look! A backgammon table—a *marble* backgammon table! And *pink* marble!"
They had gone inside for a closer look.

It was like a number of other pieces they had bought for the
house: They had seen it, decided instantly that they couldn't
live without it, and so they had paid a ridiculously high price
for it. Irene was sure that the minute the shopkeeper had seen
them—the minute the sleighbells above his door had jingled
to announce their entrance—he had seen the predatory gleam
in their eyes, heard an excited, acquisitive note in the jingling
bells, and doubled the price of the backgammon table. At least
this was what she thought at first. Later, as she discovered more
things about the table, she changed her mind and decided it had
been a bargain. The table had so many surprises in it. The raised
gallery, which ran around the edge, and the raised center bar
were not—as she had first thought—separate pieces of marble
that had been glued to the horizontal surface. The entire tabletop had been carved from a single piece of pink stone. The
twenty-four points of the backgammon game were not painted
on, as she had assumed, but were cut of alternately darker and
lighter stone and carefully inlaid.

On the day the table was delivered Justin picked up the marble top and carried it to the window. He held it up against the

light. "Look, Irene," he said. "It's almost translucent. The light shines *through*."

It was then she had noticed the hieroglyphics on the rough bottom surface—letters or numerals—and, after studying them for a long time, they had decided that part of the inscription was a date—1802.

"Just think of it," Irene said. "It's over a hundred and fifty years old."

He held it to the light again and she had begun to have the illusion of a hidden surface beneath the actual surface, of a canyoned land bathed in pink, clear sunshine that lay submerged in transparent stone.

"The color is like—like an antique pigeon's blood!" she had said, and laughed.

He lifted the marble top to replace it on its pedestal. "Be careful, Justin!" she cried. "Don't drop it!"

They had put the table between two gold chairs so that, when it was not set up for a game, it could be used to hold a cigarette dish and an ashtray. "How have we been able to live without it this long?" Irene asked. "It looks as if it had grown there!"

"It certainly ought to be a conversation piece," Justin said.

It was. Placed so prominently in the room, it called attention to itself immediately. When Irene's friends came for lunch or tea, the table provided, almost invariably, a subject for a few minutes' admiring talk. When her friends asked her, Irene said, "I'm sure there's no other in the world like it."

Neither Irene nor Justin had ever played backgammon. But, once they had the table, Irene decided they should learn. She bought a copy of a book called *Hoyle Up-To-Date,* a handsome set of black and white backgammon pieces, two pairs of dice, and two leather dice cups. As they sipped their evening coffee over the backgammon table, they studied the rules and strategy of the game. They learned that the pieces were called "stones" and that certain rolls of the dice had odd and charming names. (An opening roll of six and five allowed the player to make a move called "Lover's Leap," and a roll of six and one permitted him to make what was called his "bar point.") Irene delightedly learned that backgammon was one of the oldest games, with its origins lost in pre-Roman antiquity, and she decided that backgammon was good for them.

It was pleasant, she thought, to sit this way, on a quiet winter evening—with a fire going in the fireplace, perhaps, on snowy nights—with Justin wearing the brown velvet smoking jacket she had given him for his birthday, his feet in slippers, his pipe lighted, as they sipped her hot espresso coffee. It was a peaceful scene as she saw it—the kind of scene their lives could have used more of. They sat together, husband and wife, calmly concentrating on a single area, equally matched, with only a pair of dice to determine who would win. She was sure that Justin was as happy as she was.

When he rolled the dice for his turn, she heard the almost musical chink of the dice against the marble, and she looked deeply into the buried country. Backgammon, and the backgammon table, had, she decided, opened up a new and reassuring world to them both. For some time Irene Silton had been quietly wondering what was wrong with her marriage.

When he had finished making his move she said to him, "I learned something else from *Hoyle Up-To-Date* today."

"Did you? What?"

"There are quite a few variations on the standard game. Did you know that?"

"No," he said, "I didn't."

"Well, there are. One is called Dutch Backgammon. Then there's a game called Snake, and one called Acey-Deucey."

"Really?" he said. "That's very interesting."

"Yes. I thought, if we ever get tired of this form of the game there are all the others to try."

"Yes, that's right."

She rolled the dice for her turn. "Oh!" she said. "Lover's Leap!"

A little later she said, "Isn't this fun?"

"Yes, it is," he agreed.

"I like it because it brings us together," she said. "It gives us something to do when we're together." She smiled at him and reached for his hand across the backgammon table.

The Siltons had no children. Perhaps that was Irene's fault; perhaps it wasn't. At first, in the first years, she hadn't wanted any. She had been frightened, really, of having children. She was a small woman—a size eight—and her mother had once told her that she was not built for childbearing. On the other hand, after a while she had decided that she and Justin ought to become parents. But then nothing had happened and then, for a long time, she had urgently, wildly, wanted children. Now, she felt, they had passed a point—a critical point in marriage—where children would help, in any way, to bring them together. Though they were still young, still in their thirties, she was certain that the addition of a child now would only shatter what remained of their relationship; that, if she had a baby, Justin would leave her. Their marriage consisted now of two perilously balanced ingredients—herself and Justin—and the entrance of any third being would disrupt the balance.

What, precisely, was their marriage's illness Irene did not know. She had long since stopped trying to diagnose it and, instead, bent every effort toward preventing it from failing further. She knew—or at least she was fairly sure—that Justin still loved their house in Seventieth Street, and the furniture, each piece lovingly chosen, that the house contained. She knew there was no other woman. She knew that Justin—a successful lawyer—was doing well, and was happy, in his business. Beyond that, the reasons for their troubles were obscure and intangible. Sometimes she thought, If he would only shout at me! If he would only yell at me, abuse me, or do *something* that would define his position. But, instead of shouting, he withdrew into the silence of his smoking jacket and slippers and pipe. Instead of abuse he offered her painful considerateness and politeness. He had changed. It was hard to say how—after twelve years of marriage—but he had removed himself from her somehow. A bright, plum-colored runner ran up the stairs of their house and, for years, she had insisted that they walk up and down the stairs at the edges of the carpet, to avoid stepping on the centers of the treads where signs of wear were likeliest to show. This way they had preserved the carpet. With Justin, it seemed to her, it had come to be like that. He had developed the habit of walking up and down her edges, stepping delicately and cautiously away from the center area, as if he were trying to leave unbruised her heart's nap.

"Do you still love me?" she had asked him once, impulsively, and the instant she said the words she had known that his answer—even if it was "Yes"—would not comfort her.

"Yes, I do," he said, and Irene felt her spirit die within her, feeling his footsteps moving in their slippered way gingerly up and down her borders.

She had held herself in, fighting the hysterical urge to cry out. "Well," she said, trying to make her voice sound bright, "I love you!"

"That's good," he said.

A trifle more shrilly, she said, "I've never nagged at you, have I, the way some women do? I'm not a fuss, am I? Do I scold or criticize?"

"No," he said.

This exchange—short though it was—had exhausted her. She sat back in the sofa, limp, and closed her eyes, her head full of whirring, hopeless thoughts.

Irene believed in marriage; this was why she was determined to save her own. For years, even when she was in college, she had argued about the importance of marriage, of a man and woman in a partnership, of a mutual sharing and giving and accepting. It seemed ironic, and unfair, that her own marriage —which had begun with so much promise—should end sourly. It seemed cruel. Because, in addition to believing in marriage, she was also frightened of returning to singleness. The word "divorce" terrified her. To Irene, being unmarried meant days of waiting for invitations, hours of waiting for the telephone to ring. It meant a life of artful lies and careful pretense, of guile and insincerity, of double motives. To her, the life unmarried people lived was a dark and doubtful battleground and she, she knew, had none of the weapons, nor the courage, for the battle. She was not beautiful—she knew it. She had been called "pretty," and "pretty" in her case meant a dark-haired, small-faced, beady sort of prettiness. Alert, bright, interesting —those were the words to describe her looks. To make up for a lack of beauty she had other qualities, of course. She was efficient, tidy, an excellent housekeeper and cook, an expert financial manager, a clever hostess—but these were virtues that were useful in a married woman, not in one who was looking for a husband. One reason she wanted to keep her marriage from collapse was that she was afraid she would never have another; inside her there lurked a small, tight knot of knowledge that, if Justin had not come along when he had, she might never have married at all.

When she exploded, as she sometimes did, she screamed at him and said, "Justin, talk to me! At least talk to me! Tell me what you're thinking. Don't just sit there *trying* to look peaceful. Tell me what the trouble is! Is it me? Is there something wrong with me? Have you stopped loving me?"

He only said, "It's nothing, Irene. Please. Let me finish my paper." And she had reached a point where each vicissitude of life, each encounter with him, seemed to appear as an insurmountable wall; the future seemed to stretch ahead of her like a series of tall cliffs, each unconquerable and stern. Then, unexpectedly, walking on a Saturday morning on Lexington Avenue, she had seen something shining in the window of a dusty shop, and said, "Look, Justin—" and had taken his arm. From that moment everything began to change.

Across the backgammon table, sipping coffee one night, she said to him, "Do you remember how we used to quarrel, Justin? Just a few months ago? Do you remember how I used to scold you and accuse you of making mistakes?"

"Oh, I remember," he said.

"I admit it," she said eagerly. "I do admit it now! I was in the wrong, I know, because I suppose I *am* too fussy."

"You're very meticulous," he said.

"Thank you, but—but perhaps I was wrong to be," she said. "Anyway, have you noticed that it's different now? That we don't quarrel that way any more?"

"You're right. We don't," he said and smiled at her.

She rolled her dice out, across the tabletop, hearing their deep ring. Then she reached across and covered his hand with hers. "I love you," she said.

"And I you."

"I was thinking," she said. "About—oh, about things like the stair carpet. I've been wrong to insist that you walk up the edges of the stairs. I admit that now. I'm sorry for making you do it."

"I sometimes forget, I know," he said.

"But my point is, it's all *right* if you forget, Justin. After all, it's only a piece of carpet. It's not as important as—us, for instance."

"I agree," he said.

"And—about making you put on your slippers the minute you come in the door. You don't have to do that, either, if you don't want to."

"It's easier on the rugs with slippers."

"But I don't care! And you can smoke in the dining room, darling, from now on!"

He smiled still. "You *have* changed," he said.

"Yes," she laughed, "I know!"

It was the happiest conversation they had had in months.

"It's your turn," she said.

They returned to the game.

A little later she said, "Justin, what was it that first made you think you loved me?"

He held the dice cup in his hand, gently rattling the dice, and frowned, as he tried to think of the answer. "Do you mean what quality in you I admired most?"

"Yes," she said.

"Well, I guess it would be your executive ability," he said.

She very briefly closed her eyes. "Is that all?"

"Well, let's see—let me think."

"In the beginning, I mean," she said.

"Well—"

"Never mind. It was a silly question," she said.

"No. Wait," he said eagerly. "Remember, before we were married? We were at the Colsons' party in Englewood? I'd never danced with you before, and that night I did—I danced with you—and I thought, Irene is one of the best dancers in the world! I thought you were a wonderful dancer, considering you were such a little thing."

"Oh. Well, thank you, Justin."

"And what about you?" he asked.

"Me?"

"Yes—you, Irene."

She thought about it for a moment. "Oh, I know what it was —what I first loved about you," she said softly.

"What?"

"Before the Colsons' party. We were at my mother's place. There was a cherry tree in the garden and you took me out there, under it, and it was—oh, April, I guess, or early May, and you said—you said . . ."

"What did I say?"

"Nothing. Nothing."

"Tell me, Irene."

"Well, we were there, under the tree, and it was just beginning to flower. It was all pink, and I remember we both looked up at the blue sky between the branches of pink flowers and you took my hand in yours and you said—"

"What?"

"That I was beautiful, that's all."

"I remember now," he said.

"Yes."

"I said you were beautiful—but then you denied it."

"Did I?"

"Yes. You said that you weren't beautiful. You said that beauty wasn't as important as common sense, and you said that partnership and a mutual give-and-take were the important things in a marriage."

"What I said was true."

"So was what *I* said."

"What do you mean?"

"You were beautiful."

"Oh!" It came out as a gasp. She hated to have him see her cry—even tears of joy. To keep the tears back she opened her eyes very wide and stared hard, straight down, at the backgammon board. And, staring at it wide-eyed, she felt herself lifted into it, into the pink-lighted countryside, felt herself borne coolly down among the smooth mountains and all about her felt sunshine filtering as if through cherry blossoms.

"You've made your bar point," he said to her.

The backgammon table became the center of their lives. It was the continent that held them. It was a land that was both safe and calm. Even when they argued—as they still did upon occasion—the backgammon table was like a platform for their discussions, a lectern across which opinions flowed more easily and could be debated more sensibly.

One night she said, "Justin, do you know what I think?"

"What?" he asked her.

"This table didn't *revive* our love."

"Didn't it?"

"No. Our love was there all along. The table simply made us face each other, made us *remember* that we loved each other."

"I suppose you're right," he said.

"People," she said, "should face each other."

He looked at her. "What's the matter?" he asked her.

"Nothing—nothing," she said.

Only as they got better at the game did anything that amounted to a quarrel occur over the backgammon table. He said to her one evening, "You know, the thing I like about this game is that there's no skill involved. It's all in the way the dice land."

"Why, I think there's a lot of skill involved!" she said.

"What skill is there? I don't see any."

"There's strategy, isn't there? Don't you call strategy skill, for goodness' sake?"

"Please, Irene. Don't raise your voice at me."

"I'm not raising my voice!"

"You are. You're screaming again!"

"I'm only saying there is skill to backgammon. Your last move, for instance."

"What was wrong with it?"

"It was a very foolish move, Justin. Look, if you'd moved this stone to your three point and this one to your—"

"You always know the right move, don't you?" he said.

"As a matter of fact, I do!"

"Do you mean this move would have been better?" He rearranged his stones in the manner she had indicated.

"Yes," she said. "See? See what I mean? Look—now that stone is protected."

He studied the board. "Yes," he said finally. "You're right."

But despite such moments Irene felt that their marriage, which had been like a dying tree, was slowly beginning to flourish again over the backgammon table—that a new surge was coming to its branches, a new leafiness to its stems. And, along with her interior spring came another spring in the trees on Seventieth Street, outside her living-room windows.

"This morning," she said to him one sunny Saturday, "we have our choice. We can walk in the park or play backgammon."

"It doesn't matter," he said.

He was right, she thought comfortably, it didn't matter; whichever thing they did they would be happy doing, together.

"Well, let's play backgammon then!" she said.

"All right. You win."

"Why? Why do you say 'You win'?"

He smiled. "You usually win, don't you? At backgammon, I mean?"

She laughed. "Don't be silly!" she said. "It's because I think out my game. I use strategy!"

That evening Irene said, "Darling, do you realize what's happened? We've become so devoted to backgammon that we've neglected all our friends! I'll admit it's more fun to spend an evening alone with you but we really must have some people in —just for a change."

"All right," he said. "Who'll we have?"

"Let's have John and Eleanor Dixon."

"Fine," he said.

Irene went to the telephone. She had suggested the Dixons for a reason. Eleanor Dixon—who fancied herself an interior decorator, though she was totally without credentials—had never seen the backgammon table, and Irene was anxious to see what Eleanor thought. She invited the Dixons for the following Saturday night.

Sure enough, Eleanor had no sooner spotted the table than she marched to it. "Darling, where in the world did you get it?" she demanded.

"In a funny little shop on Lexington," Irene said.

"What shop?"

"I've forgotten the name," Irene said.

"Oh, you can't have forgotten! I *must* know."

"I don't think there's another like it in the world."

"Hey," John Dixon said, "I get it—it's like the back of a checkerboard."

"It's a backgammon table," Justin said. "Haven't you ever played backgammon?"

"We have such fun with it," Irene said. "We've got so we play backgammon night after night. It's our favorite pastime."

"Well, for heaven's sake," Eleanor Dixon said.

"It's a fascinating game, really," Irene said. "And highly skilled. It's one of the oldest games there is. No one knows how old, exactly, it is, but they played backgammon in the days of the Roman Empire."

"You don't say."

"I call the color antique pigeon's blood," Irene said. "Isn't it an old, *old* looking pink? The table is over a hundred and fifty years old itself. The marble was probably quarried in Algeria and the stone has a date on the back of it that looks like 1802."

Eleanor knelt to examine the carved letters and numbers on the underside.

"Here," Justin said, "I'll show you—"

"Don't lift it, Justin," Irene said.

"I can see the lettering," Eleanor said.

"I want to show you how translucent it is," Justin said. "Here, let me hold it up to the light."

"Please don't lift it, Justin!" Irene said. "You'll drop it."

"I won't drop it. I want to show Eleanor—"

"No—"

He started to lift it, and at the same time she reached out to restrain him. For a brief moment they struggled over it—one raising the table upward and the other pressing it down—and so, when it fell, suddenly, from their hands and crashed to the floor it seemed impossible that they had done it together and yet, at the same time, they knew that they had.

Irene looked blankly at the broken marble and then cried out as if the jagged mountains and canyons she had seen beneath its surface had collapsed upon her and stabbed her. "Oh, you idiot!" she screamed. "You stupid, clumsy fool! You did it!"

He stood facing her, his hands trembling. *"You,"* he said. "You did it! You did it, just as you've done everything else. You destroyed it, just as you've destroyed everything, always! Always arranging, planning, dominating everything—it's you! It's you who've broken everything, always!"

"Oh, no!" She sank to her knees, sobbing, picked up the scattered pieces of broken marble and crushed them to her bosom. "Oh, God!" she cried. "I can't bear to live without it!"

"Oh, dear, dear—" Eleanor Dixon whispered.

"Maybe you can find another like it, Irene," John Dixon said lamely.

But they did not find another like it.

It turned out to be insured under one of the policies the Siltons maintained on their home and property, and after a week or two Justin told Irene that he put in a claim for the cost of the table. "I guess that makes me feel a little better about it," he said. "It's good to get money *back* from the insurance company for a change."

Irene said nothing.

At Abercrombie & Fitch she bought a folding wooden backgammon board. It did not have the cool feel of the marble table, of course, and it produced no clear and true ring when the dice were cast upon it, as the other had. In other ways, too, it was not at all the same. It was more awkward than the table had been because, when they held it on their laps, or between them on the yielding sofa cushions, the stones had a tendency to slide about and become disarranged and the board itself had a tendency to double up on them, suddenly, in the middle of a game. They were forever, it seemed, starting over from the beginning. And, because the board was made of birch and not marble, it contained no buried mountain scenery.

Irene did not mention the marble table again, until one night, several weeks later, when the board folded up, the stones scattering, and she rose from the sofa and walked quickly to the place in the room where the table had stood. She put both hands out for it, as though it might still be there, invisibly and indestructibly shining.

He did not look up at her. "What's the matter?" he asked her.

"I loved it so!" she said. And then, "Where did we go wrong, Justin? Was it me?"

For a moment or two he said nothing. Then he said, "If it makes you feel any better, the marble wasn't from Algeria. It was from Massachusetts. The insurance company sent an appraiser—for the claim. We were overcharged for the table. It wasn't an antique, either. It was only three or four years old."

"Oh," she said. "I see."

"Or perhaps that doesn't make you feel any better."

"Well—"

"Well—" he said. He had begun to set up the board again. "Let's play the game," he said. He rolled the dice. "I've just made my bar point," he said.

She returned to the sofa and sat down before the board.

They played in silence now.

It was not just that the table had deceived her, she thought; it went deeper than that. The thing the table had stood for had deceived her. The love that she had thought was so alive and springing was, in fact, long dead. How long dead she did not know but it certainly had died before the day they had stood outside the shop on Lexington Avenue and had seen the table laden with empty picture frames. It had died, perhaps, even before the Colsons' party in Englewood, and yet it had been alive that afternoon under the cherry tree at her mother's place. Somewhere in the time between then and now it had died. Who knew when it had died? Or did the date really matter? The death had been quiet, discreet, unheralded. And the backgammon table had been nothing more than a marble monument to that dead love.

RACE DAY

✾✾✾✾ Close to eleven o'clock Mr. and Mrs. Foley got to the club, parking the car down near the bathhouses. As Mr. Foley flicked off the ignition switch the starting gun for the race went off. Mrs. Foley plugged her ears with her fingers and remarked, "Goodness, you'd think it was a bombing or something, to hear the noise. It was deafening, just absolutely deafening." Mr. Foley got out of the car and said, "C'mon, for gosh sake, do you want to miss the whole thing? My gosh, we're late already!" He slammed the car door shut and started across the gravel drive toward the clubhouse.

They both were in their early forties. Mrs. Foley was small, with crisply curled reddish hair and freckled arms. She wore a white tennis dress and white canvas shoes. Mr. Foley, a heavy man, wore a white visored cap, a blue pullover sweater, and yachting pants that were dirty and patched around the knees. "Wait for me, dear," Mrs. Foley said, hurrying to catch up with him. Mr. Foley took his wife's arm and steered her purposefully up the front steps of the clubhouse, through the lounge, and out the French doors toward the line of white benches in front of the pier. It was one of those warm, clear mornings on

Long Island Sound when the windows of the club were always thrown wide open, and the combination of the fine day and the race had brought out quite a crowd of members. Deck chairs had been scattered across the stone terrace, even on the pier. All heads were turned toward the water. The judges, with heavy binoculars slung over their shoulders, were gathered at the far end of the pier, their white trousers and white shirts gleaming in the sunlight. Mr. and Mrs. Foley finally found an empty bench.

"There they go!" said Mr. Foley. "Look at the *Penguin*. What a boat!"

"What a boat!" Mrs. Foley echoed.

The Lightning Class was racing.

Mrs. Foley sat down beside her husband. "I'm wondering," she said. "Do you want red diamonds with white crisscross or white diamonds with red crisscross? I can do either." She started to open her knitting bag.

"Whichever is easiest for you, dear," Mr. Foley said, not looking at her.

"Well, now, don't say that," said Mrs. Foley. "Say something definite so I'll have something definite to go on. I can't go ahead at random and do just *anything*."

"Uh-huh," said Mr. Foley. Then, turning to her, he added crossly, "Don't knit now, Grace. Do you want everybody to get the idea you don't give a hoot about the races?"

"Well," Mrs. Foley said, "you know, I really *don't* give a hoot about the races. You know that. Not actually. Besides, I don't see why I can't knit and watch them at the same time."

"Uh-huh," said Mr. Foley. "Well, I think it looks kind of funny."

Someone said, "Hello, Jim. Hello, Grace."

"Why, hello, Frank," Mr. Foley said, standing up.

"Good morning," said Mrs. Foley.

"How's your wife, Frank?"

"Just fine, Jim. How're you two?" He looked at Mrs. Foley. "I haven't seen you around here in a long time."

"Well—" Mrs. Foley began.

"I've been down," Mr. Foley interrupted, "but Grace was on the sick list. She hasn't been down lately."

"Oh, I'm sorry," Frank said.

"Oh, I haven't been sick really," Mrs. Foley said. "I had my spring cold in April, but it's just that I don't care much for sailing. I mean, I don't pretend to understand all the rules—starboard tacks and handicaps and everything. It's all Greek to me."

"Well, you've really been neglecting us," said Frank. "You coming to the Sailors' Dinner?"

"No, I don't believe so," Mrs. Foley said.

"Why, sure we're coming," said Mr. Foley. "We wouldn't want to miss that, would we, Grace?"

"Well," said Mrs. Foley, "I'll have to see. Just when is that, Frank?"

"It's on the club calendar, Grace—the twenty-second. Gosh, Jim, you two haven't been getting your dues' worth out of this place. Well . . ."

Mr. Foley laughed. "Guess you're right, Frank," he said.

"Got to be pushing along," Frank said. "Nice to see you again. Got to get back to the wife."

"Nice to see you," said Mrs. Foley.

"See you around, Frank," said Mr. Foley.

When he had left them, Mrs. Foley reached into her knitting bag and took out her glasses. They were tinted green and gold-framed. Mr. Foley sat down heavily beside her. "You going to wear *those?*" he asked sharply. "You know you look like the devil in those."

"Yes, I know," said Mrs. Foley, "but I can't read without them. I was going to do a crossword puzzle."

"What are you going to do a crossword puzzle for?"

"Well, I've been putting off doing it," Mrs. Foley said.

"Ye gods, Grace!"

"What's the matter?"

"What do you mean, what's the matter? Do you mean to say you're going to sit here and do a crossword puzzle while the race is going on? Don't you give a darn what people think about you?"

"Of course I do, but—"

"Ye gods," he said, "if you don't care what people think about *you,* you might at least think of what people think about me. Ye gods, right in front of Frank Hillman you said—"

"Oh," she said, *"that's* who that was. For the life of me, I couldn't think of his last name."

"Frank Hillman? You couldn't think of *Frank Hillman?*" He struck his forehead with the heel of his palm. "He's only the new commodore of the club, that's all! Ye gods!"

"Please don't keep saying 'ye gods,' dear."

"Quite an impression you must have made on him! Incidentally, when I said you'd been sick why did you contradict me? He's the most important man in the club. You know darn well he'll think it's funny."

"Why should he think it's funny?" Mrs. Foley asked. "Besides, I haven't been sick, and I don't see why—"

"Look," he said, "couldn't you see he thought it was funny you don't come down here more often? You know the way that wife of his talks. You know she'll think it's funny. They'll get the idea you don't like the club."

"Oh, I do like the club," Mrs. Foley said. "It would be silly of them to get the idea that I don't like the club."

"Then you'd better come to the Sailors' Dinner. It's the twenty-second. Gosh, you should have known that!"

"It must have slipped my mind," she said. "I guess I just hadn't planned on going."

"Look," he said, "I'm pretty well thought of here, you can tell that. There's a good chance I'll be put on the board of governors next year. But you act like you're deliberately trying to ruin all my chances."

"Now, now," Mrs. Foley said consolingly, "you know that isn't true."

His eyes turned toward the water again. "The *Penguin* is still out in front," he said. "There she goes. That's the Pitcairns' boat. They'll get the cup this year, wait and see."

Mrs. Foley watched the boats for a moment or two. Then she reached into her knitting bag and took out a folded section of the newspaper and a pencil. She studied the page. "Oh, dear," she said. "Current affairs. I don't know a thing about current affairs."

"Hmm," said Mr. Foley, his eyes still on the boats. "What about 'em?"

"That's the subject of the crossword puzzle. Every week they have a different subject."

He turned and glared at her. "So you're going to do it!"

"Oh, please," she said. "Nobody's paying any attention to us. Please let me do it. I brought it out here to do."

He turned away, not answering her. "Hey!" he said. "Look—

they're coming about now. Roddie Pitcairn's the skipper of that boat. Good little skipper, too."

"Is he the one at Harvard?"

"No, Dartmouth."

"Oh, yes."

Mrs. Foley concentrated on her puzzle and Mr. Foley crossed his legs and leaned forward, watching the boats.

"Can you think of a six-letter word meaning 'cabinet,' Jim?" Mrs. Foley asked after a moment.

"Bureau," said Mr. Foley. "Does that fit?"

"Perhaps," Mrs. Foley said. "But then seventeen across doesn't work. I'll have to see . . ."

"Why, hi there!" a girl's voice said.

"Ruth," he said, "how are you? Ruthie, you know my wife, Mrs. Foley? Grace, this is Ruthie Pitcairn. This is Roddie Pitcairn's sister."

"How do you do?" Mrs. Foley smiled.

"Why, how do you do?" the girl said. She was perhaps eighteen, with long, tanned legs below her blue sailcloth shorts. A striped blazer was across her shoulders.

"We've been watching the races," Mrs. Foley said.

"Aren't they exciting?" Ruth Pitcairn said, tossing her head. "You know, I've lost my lighter. That's why I came over. You haven't seen it, have you? It's silver with my initials on it."

Mrs. Foley looked around her on the bench, on the terrace beneath her feet. "Why, no, we haven't," she said. "Can you remember where you had it last?"

"No, I can't," the girl said. "Isn't that silly of me? Well, if you should see it . . ."

"Oh, we'll let you know," Mrs. Foley said.

"The *Penguin* is doing just fine," said Mr. Foley. "Just fine."

"Yes, it is, isn't it," said the girl.

"Your brother's a fine little skipper, yessiree. He'll get the cup this year."

"He's doing splendidly," said Ruth. "I'm so thrilled. Well," she said, "it was awfully nice to meet you, Mrs. Foley. Hope I'll see you again soon. Are you coming to the Sailors' Dinner?"

"Well . . ." Mrs. Foley began.

"Sure thing," Mr. Foley said quickly. "We'll be there."

"I hope so," Mrs. Foley said.

"Good. Well, if you should see my lighter . . ."

"We'll be on the lookout," Mrs. Foley said.

When they were alone again Mrs. Foley said, "My, isn't she pretty? How did you meet her, Jim?"

"Ruth? She took the junior tennis championship last summer. Nice girl. You'd meet people too, Grace, if you'd come here more often."

"She was wearing a fraternity pin of some sort," Mrs. Foley said. "I think it was Psi Omega. My, don't girls get engaged young these days!"

"It wasn't Psi Omega," Mr. Foley said. "I don't know what it was, but it wasn't Psi Omega."

"If we had a daughter I'd like to have her look exactly like that," Mrs. Foley said. "Exactly like that."

"Uh-huh."

Mrs. Foley looked back at her puzzle.

"Pitcairn's going to get this race," Mr. Foley said. "Just look at that. That boat is perfectly handled. Ha! There's Joe Winter's boat way behind. Boy, that does my heart good."

"Mm, yes," said Mrs. Foley.

"What a race, what a race! They're doing the long course to-day."

"Isn't it warm!" Mrs. Foley said.

"Stan Pitcairn owns one of the biggest paper mills in Connecticut. They live in Old Greenwich. I hear they have quite a mansion up there."

Mrs. Foley nodded.

"Did I tell you Joe Winter wanted to draw up a contract with our firm?" Mr. Foley asked. "Boy, I wouldn't trust him as far as I could throw him. Now, Pitcairn's another matter. I've been getting pretty buddy-buddy with Pitcairn lately, and one of these days I'm going to put the proposition to him. That's why I want you to play up to the Pitcairns at the Sailors' Dinner."

"But I don't know them at all," Mrs. Foley said.

"You will. I'll introduce you at the Sailors' Dinner."

"Jim," she said softly, "I don't really want to go to the Sailors' Dinner."

He looked at her. "Why not?"

"Jim," she said, "I don't really know any of these people. I guess you'd say I'm shy. And quite frankly, dear, I don't like a lot of them."

"Huh?" he said. "In one breath you say you don't know them; in the next you say you don't like them. What kind of sense does that make?"

"The ones I've met, I mean," she said.

"Why don't you like 'em, for gosh sake?"

Mrs. Foley thought a moment. "I don't think they're sincere," she said finally.

"What do you mean 'sincere'?"

"By sincere I mean *sincere*. I mean, so many of them seem to feel they've got to be friendly to me just because I'm a member of the club, not because they like me."

"Look, Grace," he said, "if you'd just put yourself out more —like me—they'd like you. Look at me. Why, I guess you'd say I was one of the best-liked guys in the club. It's because I'm— well, I'm friendly. I don't bury my nose in a crossword puzzle."

"Oh, I know, I know," Mrs. Foley said.

Just then a woman passed them, glanced at them, then turned and started back toward them. "Grace and Jim!" the woman said. "How wonderful to see you! Isn't this a glorious day?"

"How are you?" said Mrs. Foley.

Mr. Foley stood up. "Molly!" he said. "My, you look more beautiful every day."

"Flatterer!" the woman said. "Isn't the race exciting? That darling Pitcairn boy—isn't he a wonder?"

"He certainly is," Mrs. Foley said. "We were just remarking—"

"We're all going down to the beach to watch the finish," the woman said. "Why don't you come down with us? Stan and Louise Pitcairn are down there already."

"Oh, I'm afraid we've got to be going soon," Mrs. Foley said.

"Say, that sounds great," Mr. Foley said. "We'll be right down."

"Good!" the woman said. "Quick, slip into your swim suits and meet us on the beach." The woman hurried off.

Mr. Foley remained standing. "C'mon, Grace," he said, "let's change."

She looked at him imploringly. "Oh, Jim, must we?"

"Grace, for gosh sake, come on. Look, the Pitcairns are down there!"

"But it will mean we'll have to stay for lunch—"

"So what? Come on."

Mrs. Foley picked up her pencil and hurriedly wrote "b-u-r-e-a-u" in the empty squares. She folded the paper and put it in her bag. She stood up and looked across the water. The sails of the Lightnings seemed suddenly loaded, sagging, filled with the stillness of the day. Standing up gave her the impression that the boats were now standing absolutely still.

"Come on."

She followed her husband back through the clubhouse, out toward the bathhouses. At the door to the women's section they separated. Mrs. Foley walked down the open corridor to her dressing room and stepped inside. Her bathing suit and cap were hanging on the hook inside. She began to undress. Of course Jim was right, she thought. She did not try. She did not put herself out. She failed him at every turn. And yet—and yet— Well, she would try once more. She got into her bathing suit and sat down on the hard wooden bench to put on her shoes. Through the thin partition she heard the sound of the door to the next room being unlocked, then opened. There was a mumble of feminine voices and laughter. Suddenly one voice rose above the other. It was Ruthie Pitcairn's.

"Guess where I found it," Ruthie was saying. "Mr. Foley was sitting on it—it was on their bench. It was under his fat ass the whole time. As soon as they got up to leave I saw it there. Fasten my bra strap, will you?"

" *'They'?*" said the other voice. "Who are 'they'?"

"His wife, of course. Who else?"

"You mean there's someone who would actually *marry* that old fart? *C'est incroyable!*"

"And they're perfectly matched," Ruthie said. "A computer couldn't have done a better job."

Mrs. Foley didn't move. She wanted to get up and run out, but she couldn't move.

"What's she like?"

"Like him—a bore. But at least she's *quiet*. Have you ever *listened* to that man? Pretending to be such a sailing buff, calling everybody 'skipper,' and 'mate,' walking around in those dirty old sailor pants, looking like a horse's rear end? Daddy says it's a wonder they ever let him in the club. Ask Daddy to tell you about the time he—"

Mrs. Foley shut her ears. She became conscious suddenly of a big bluebottle fly that buzzed noisily about the room. She noticed that there was a smell in the air, like bacon frying, from the clubhouse kitchen. In her nostrils that bacon smell seemed to grow until it was almost overpowering, and the sound of the buzzing fly seemed unbearable. She felt stifled, ill, suffocated by the smothering smell, the sound of the fly, the heat of the day, the closeness of the dressing room. Something was happening inside her. A hot arrow of pain was moving slowly through her, piercing one by one all the chambers of her heart. I can't get up, she thought. I'm rooted here.

After a while she heard the door of the other dressing room open again and close, and the sound of voices and footsteps recede along the corridor. She stood up and opened the door.

One end of the corridor opened upon a short flight of wooden steps that led down to the beach. From the top of the steps she saw her husband. He was in his bathing trunks, still wearing his visored cap, talking animatedly to the two couples on the beach.

He looked up and saw her, excused himself, and started toward her.

At the foot of the steps she met him. She wanted suddenly to take him in her arms, to cradle him as she might a child, to say to him, "Oh, my dear, it doesn't matter. You're not that kind of man. Not to me." He took her arm and whispered, "That tall fellow's Pitcairn. His wife's the woman in the blue suit. Be nice to them."

She gave him her brightest smile. "I've been thinking," she said. "Shall I ask them to join our table at the Sailors' Dinner?"

He pinched her elbow. "Atta girl!" he said. "I knew you'd come to your senses. Atta girl!"

WE LUCKY GENIUSES

✿✿✿✿ "Do you know what day this is?" she asked him. They were driving down the Coast Highway, heading south from Carmel. The sun was indulging itself—really overdoing it a bit, he thought—setting flashily into the sea on their right, capping the waves with fiery points and turning the sky all the colors of a ribbon counter. But he had been intent not so much upon the sun's California behavior as upon the lanes of automobiles before and behind him. And in his mind he had been weaving lines to be carved on his headstone, in case there should be, as the radio had said, thirty-six more traffic deaths that weekend and his number should be included among them.

He asked her to repeat the question. And when she did he simply said no, annoyed at having his happy, mortuary thoughts interrupted. He had been writing for his epitaph: "Devoted husband, good provider, loyal friend"—things like that—and "Had love the pow'r to stay the hand of death!" while ticking off in his head the names of all the people in the world who loved him.

"It's September twentieth," she said.

"Oh?" Noncommittally.

"It's a year. A year is up tonight."

"Well, well!" he said. And then, "I guess you're right. At midnight." He glanced at her. She looked very tanned, very decorative in the open car with her wavy blonde hair blowing. She spread her slim fingers from the open window, moving them as if she were groping for a chord on a piano or trying to seize the sun's last rays. But her next words dispelled that illusion.

"Good-by!" she said, and he realized that she was doing nothing more poetic than waving a childish farewell to the sun. "I can't wait for it to be midnight," she said, and he wondered if one of his mistakes hadn't been marrying a girl six years younger than he.

"Uh-huh," he said. He drove faster. "I'm sure the Parkers' party won't last that long."

"But if it does," she asked, "shall we announce it to everyone?"

"Sure," he said. "Why not? What will you say?"

She turned to him. "I'll say," she said pleasantly, "that a year ago today, September twenty-first, I promised my husband solemnly—after he'd begged me for days and weeks and months to promise him solemnly—I'd stick it out for another year."

"I see," he said. "And what if they ask you what you're going to do now?"

"I'll say that because absolutely nothing has changed and, having stuck out my year through thick and thin, mostly thin, I've decided to go free, as free as a bird. Off on my own, to find out what the good life really is like. And that tomorrow morning will see me packing my bags."

"Very good," he said. "Very well put."

"Thank you," she said.

They drove in silence. He had forgotten that promise, that bargain, or whatever it was they had made a year ago. Except that he had not really forgotten, only pushed it back into a little mental closet he kept specifically for old, unpleasant pacts, contracts he had been forced to sign, things he had had to compromise about or beg for. Of course he remembered it now though he had not remembered the exact date. It was like her to remember the date, and it was also like her not to have mentioned it to him since then or let him know she had been counting the days, as if the period were a prison sentence. It was funny, really, to realize that for the last three hundred and sixty-five days she had been quietly going about the ritual of living but biding her time.

"How cute of you to remember."

She laughed softly. "I haven't had much else to think about."

After a moment he said, "You know, I really thought things were going pretty well."

"I'm sure you did," she said. "Oh, look, Hugh! Look at the sun now."

He looked. Only a bright tip showed, and the sky above it was Chinese red. "Pretty," he said, looking back at the road.

"Don't drive so fast."

"We're going to be late as it is."

"I wish it weren't the Parkers. I hate the Parkers."

"That's right. I'd forgotten you hate the Parkers. It's very helpful, darling, having you hate the Parkers, since you know he's considering a script of mine."

"I know," she said. "But that's been one of my troubles all along. I've never been able to like people I utterly despise. Pomposity and arrogance I think I could forgive him, even when he tries to kiss me, if he didn't try to do it in such a pompous, arrogant way."

"Well, I'm sure Ed Parker will enjoy the little announcement you're planning to make at midnight."

"Yes," she said. "But if he should appear too interested, I shall have to add that Ed Parker, alas, is not for me."

"You're doing very well," he said. "You should have been the writer and not I."

"A number of people have said that somebody else should be the writer and not you."

"Why, thank you, Lucille! You're always so very, very sweet."

"Don't mention it."

"Tell me," he said. "All those days and weeks and months when I supposedly begged you to stick it out another year—and frankly I don't remember begging you quite that long—what made you decide to stay?"

"Don't you remember?"

"I'm afraid I don't."

"Well," she said, "it was like all the other times I've agreed to stay."

"What do you mean?"

"It was because I thought, Heel that he is most of the time, every now and then he does something wonderful."

"Those lines," he said, "sound just as fresh as when they were written by Oscar Hammerstein."

"I'm sorry," she said, "but that was what I thought."

"And what was the wonderful thing I did a year ago?"

"It was something you said."

"What did I say?"

"I've forgotten."

"Lucille—"

"Please. I don't want to talk about it any more."

He looked at her again. Her right arm trailed out the window, her left hand reposed in her lap, but there was something rigid about her whole pose, something hard and resolute in the set of her shoulders. Her face was turned away from him.

"Nine years is a long time," he said finally.

"I know," she said. "Very long."

"You'd think that in such a long time we might have learned something."

"Oh, I have," she said. "I've learned a great deal."

"What have you learned?"

"I've learned all about geniuses." And she added, "Or should it be genii?"

"Genii are what you get when you rub magic lamps," he said.

She laughed dryly. "That's hilarious, Hugh."

"Give me a minute and I'll think of something better. Tell me more about geniuses. What have you learned about them?"

She leaned back against the leather seat. "Oh," she said, "I've learned that gifted, talented—geniuses, really, like you, are erratic and unpredictable. They have temper tantrums and have to be comforted like babies. You have to pamper a genius or he sulks."

"I see. And what else?"

"I've learned that gifted, talented geniuses like you are extremely selfish and demanding and expect the world to revolve around them."

"Yes."

"And I've learned that people like you, who write fantastically funny comedies, who were put in the world to make audiences hold their sides with laughter, who can come up with twenty-four brand-new gags a day, are really, deep inside—

what is the cliché?—clowns with breaking hearts. And that people like you, who can put everybody at a cocktail party in
stitches, actually have great big bleeding, babyish souls."

"Very good! Excellent!" he said.

"And that people like you," she went on, "feel cruelty and
smallness can be forgiven because you're talented. The world
has to overlook your fits of bad temper. And your sulks. Even
your fibs. Just because you're sometimes very humorous. And
I've learned that—"

"You're really wound up," he said. "Go on."

"And I've learned that when people like you promise that
someday you're going to do something *great* and *important* and
honest and—your own cliché—'contribute to the great library
of human culture,' that when people like you say things like
that, it sounds very pretty but it never happens. Because people
like you are really flops."

"Flops? Do you really think so?"

"Yes."

"I wouldn't say you'd done too badly, Lucille," he said
easily. "You've got a maid, a mink, a house in Pebble Beach."

"Oh, lord!" she said. "Is that the way you measure success?
A house in Pebble Beach, a maid, and a mink! Besides, I never
asked for those things. You just presented them to me."

"You mean you didn't want them?"

"Not really."

"You've had good use out of some of those things."

She didn't seem interested any more. "I know." And then
she said, "Hugh, let's not talk about it. I'm sorry I started it—
truly I am."

"You were brave," he said, "to put up with it all for nine
years."

"Oh, look!" she said. "Look at the gulls, how low they're flying! Look at that one swoop!"

He looked at the birds against the fading sky. He reached down and turned on the low-beam headlights. "I wish you could remember," he said.

"Remember what?"

"What it was I said a year ago."

"Oh," she said. "Well, as a matter of fact, I do remember."

"What was it?"

"I'm sorry. I don't want to spoil it by repeating it to you."

"I see."

"It was one of the few rather sweet things you've ever said. That's another thing about people like you, about geniuses. You're very lucky; the right thing pops into your head at just the right moment, and you say it. Your whole life can be about to collapse around you, and something steps in and saves the day. It's almost uncanny, the narrow escapes that geniuses have —by sheer fool's luck."

"If I could remember the lucky thing I said, I'd say it again now," he said softly.

"You'd put it into the script, you mean."

"No, I—"

"Don't bother," she said. "This script, this particular script, is over. We can't use another installment."

"Well, you know me," he said. "I always love a happy ending."

"It's not in the cards for this one, I'm afraid."

"Too bad," he said. "I had such high hopes."

He felt her look at him again, then look away. He thought, Perhaps she was right; perhaps he had been writing this script for too long. Possibly he had been writing too much of it by himself and had been resisting her collaboration. But surely it was too late now to go back over their marriage and make revisions.

The trouble was, he was not a genius. He knew that. Smart, yes. Clever, yes. Resourceful, good at keeping his eye on the main chance. He was all those things, but not a genius. Of course, he had been called a genius before. Genius is perhaps the cheapest word in show business. "Hugh Martin is a genius." "Call in Hugh Martin; he'll save the script. The guy's a genius." He'd heard it over and over again; but, he thought wryly, at least he was smart enough not to believe it. As for the other part—well, she was wrong there, too. He had it in him. Someday he *would* contribute to the great library of human culture. There was plenty of time. It was still early; he was only thirty-five. The big thing, the important thing, would come in due course. He'd planned his life pretty well so far; it had gone off without too many hitches. He'd plan the rest, too, and find a slot for everything.

He knew how things should be. Life is like a poker game; to get through it successfully requires certain dodges, a certain manner, a sense of situation, knowing when to bluff and when to play it straight. He had tried to teach her how things should be, which included how to dress, how to use makeup, how to talk, and how to mix a memorable cocktail. But on the whole she had been a reluctant student. That, essentially, always had been the difficulty between them. "You criticize me," she said. But of course, he criticized her! He *had* to criticize her, didn't he, when she made mistakes?

Suddenly sad, he remembered Lucille's little attempts to show that perhaps she, too, knew how things should be. At parties, for instance, she would be solemn when everyone else was being witty, and when the conversation was serious she would make jokes. And her jokes, he often had told her flatly, did not come off; her timing was all wrong. Be charming without trying to be funny, he had told her again and again. Her little failures embarrassed him. She had a habit of forgetting to freshen her lipstick and of forgetting to zip the last inch of zipper on the back of her dress—little things, but they were important, weren't they? Of course. She made grammatical mistakes. She tried so hard to play her part that she was pathetic in it, so pathetic and awkward that he was forever having to think up lines to cover her mistakes.

But worst of all, of course, was the way she sometimes managed, with a thoughtless word, to deflate the small balloon of confidence that he liked to keep blown up around him. And when this happened— Well, he thought, perhaps I have a few faults, too.

The sun was gone; a strip of far horizon was in a final blaze of Technicolor; he was driving very fast. He thought, But the point is, I do love her.

Perhaps he was a heel. Probably no other woman in the world would have put up with him for nine whole years, and for this alone he loved her. Of course, just because she had put up with him did not mean she loved him. Yet for a time, when they first were married, it had seemed as if she did. He thought of those early weeks, when they'd been gay together. She loved the sea, the sky, the earth, just being outdoors. They had spent days on the beach, driving in the hills, picnicking in the woods—like happy children. That was it. She had been so young, only twenty then. But he couldn't play forever. And so, for years—those carefree days were long past—she had merely lived with him patiently, putting up with him. How could he expect her to love him? Yes, that one point, that tiny but significant point, had been left out of the script. If he had the script to do over again he would put that in somehow. And all at once, desperately, he knew that he couldn't live without her. She had come to fill too deep a cavity within him.

"Perhaps," he said, "if we had had children—"

"Perhaps," she said, "perhaps not. It's too late now."

"Not too late to have children."

"No, but too late to *want* them. That's the big thing. For nine years we haven't wanted them. Or, rather, you haven't. You can't start wanting things like children this late."

"Perhaps if there hadn't been so many parties. Things like that."

"There are a lot of perhaps."

"I love you, Lucille."

"Ah, Hugh," she said earnestly, "I believe you. I know you love me in your own funny way. But—"

Suddenly something struck the front fender of the car. She screamed, *"Hugh!"*

He pressed the brake pedal hard.

"You hit something!" she cried.

"Wait here," he said. He opened the door and stepped out. He walked slowly back on the edge of the highway, searching along the dark roadside. At last he saw it—a sea gull lying on the asphalt shoulder. He went to it, knelt, and touched it. Its wing jerked slightly under his hand. He picked it up. The bird was limp and surprisingly heavy. He carried it back to the car. "Look," he said softly.

"Oh, a gull!" she cried. "Oh, the poor thing!"

"It's alive," he said. "And I think its wings are all right." Gently he placed it on the seat of the car.

"Hugh," she said, "what are you going to do with it?"

He got into the car.

"Leave it by the road, for heaven's sake, Hugh!"

He said nothing and started the motor.

"Hugh, if this is going to be one of your jokes, taking a sea gull to the Parkers' party, don't, please! It's not funny—it's horrible!"

He swung the car out into the road again and made a wide U turn, heading back the way they had come.

"Hugh, what in the world are you doing?" Her voice was tearful.

"Quiet! Be quiet," he snapped. He reached for the gull beside him on the seat and lifted it to his lap. He drove very fast. It was six miles back to the house, but he made it in fewer minutes. He turned into the driveway, stopped the car, got out, and ran up the steps, carrying the bird.

The house was empty, immaculate, filled only with serene white furniture. Lucille's high heels followed him across the polished floor.

"Get me a medicine dropper," he said. "Quick."

She ran out, carrying the dropper. He seized it. Cradling the gull in the crook of his left elbow, he lifted the stopper from the whiskey decanter. He jabbed the medicine dropper into the bottle and withdrew a few drops. Then he pressed the bird's bill open firmly with his fingers. Slowly, a drop at a time, he trickled the whiskey into the bird's mouth. Then he waited. Standing tensely beside him, Lucille waited too.

The gull's eyes fluttered open. Hugh took the bird to the wide glass door and carried it onto the high terrace that overlooked the sea. He raised the bird on the palm of his hand and held it outstretched for several moments. Suddenly, with a leap and a flash of wings, the gull rose and soared away into the night.

Lucille sobbed, "Oh, thank God!" and sat down hard on one of the terrace chairs, her face in her hands.

"Come on, let's go," he said gruffly. "We're going to be late."

She stood up and followed him to the car.

"When I was a kid," he said, "I used to love birds. They were a hobby." He started the car. "It was a funny kind of hobby, I guess. The other kids used to call me Birdbrain." He laughed softly. "They were jealous because I was the smartest kid in class. So they called me Birdbrain and left me alone with my birds."

They headed south again, faster than ever, because now they were going to be very late indeed, and he tried to think about Ed Parker and the funny script he wanted Ed to buy.

After a while he said, "Nine years," and paused. "Look, Lucille, suppose we take a trip somewhere—how about that? How about Mexico? You always loved Mexico. Or Hawaii. What do you think of that, Lucille? I mean, my lord, Lucille, nine years! There must have been *something* to keep us together that long. Look, suppose we sell the house? I mean it. Suppose we move out into the valley? Or suppose we go south?"

"No, no," she said softly. "That isn't what I want to know."

"What, then?"

"It wasn't—it wasn't just part of a script, just then, back at the house, was it? You didn't do that, did you, just because —just because you thought the story needed a tender scene?"

He glanced at her. Her head was back against the leather upholstery, and she was looking straight up at the sky that flew by above them, and her eyes seemed stabbed with stars.

Then quickly she said, "No, don't answer. I know it wasn't

that. I'm sorry I said it." He felt her hand touch his arm. "Nine years," she said. "Shall we try for ten?"

He started to say something; then a memory stopped him. It was a memory of himself not as a boy who loved birds but as a man not so long ago. He had been in his study, talking on the telephone, having an argument with a producer. The producer had wanted some changes in a script, involving lines that Hugh had written for the leading woman character. Hugh had been against the changes and had said, "No, no. . . . No, she's not that kind of woman! She wouldn't say that. Sure, she's beautiful and warm and tender, but she's got something else, too. A kind of spark, an intelligence, a quality of nobility. She's not just a lovely mannequin; she's a very real woman—someone like Lucille!" And as he had said that he had turned and seen Lucille standing in the doorway. It had been just a year ago.

He couldn't help thinking of what she had said about geniuses—that they seemed to have, when they needed it, a kind of fool's luck. It was a shocking thought. But for the first time in his life he began to wonder whether, indeed, he *was* one.

BRIGHT, YOUNG FACES

Acapulco, Mexico, January 29

✥✥✥✥ Today should have been one of the happiest days of my life. Instead, it has been a jumble. I can't sleep. Sally is sitting now, tailor-fashion, on one of the twin beds across the room from me. The money, all of it, is still spread out in the folds of her skirt. She can't sleep either, but for a different reason.

We have been at this hotel for three days; it was to have been the last stop on our honeymoon. We have come from Mexico City, Cuernavaca, and Taxco. We had planned to fly back home to Chicago tomorrow morning. Next week I was to begin practicing law in Evanston. But tonight the plans have changed.

We have been married exactly two weeks. This evening, to celebrate our two weeks' anniversary, we went to the night club in the hotel for dinner. It is a large, pleasant room with a wide outdoor terrace and dance floor. After dinner Sally and I danced for quite a while. We have always danced well together. We are both small. Sally, in high heels, is just a shade shorter than I am, and that is ideal for dancing. Suddenly, the master of ceremonies announced an elimination dance. Throughout the dance, he explained, the poorest dancers would be eliminated one by one by the judges, until finally only the two best couples would be left on the floor. Then, judging by the applause from the tables, the best couple would be selected. The prize was a bottle of champagne.

Sally and I almost didn't get involved in it. We started to sit down, but then Sally said, "Oh, let's do it," so we did. We danced all our fanciest steps, all our dips and twirls, until finally Sally and I, and one other couple, were left on the floor. Everybody clapped for us and we were given the bottle of champagne.

They pushed a microphone over to us and asked us to say a few words. But for some reason, instead of saying simply, "Thank you," Sally began to make a little speech. I don't know what made her say some of the things she did. Perhaps even then, at that point, she had some uncanny knowledge of what would happen. But she began talking, telling the people in the room that we were just married ("As if we couldn't guess!" someone shouted), that we were from Chicago, that we wished we could stay forever in Acapulco—it was so beautiful—but, alas, that we had to leave tomorrow for home. She told them that I was just out of law school, that I was going back to start my own practice "in a little cubbyhole of an office," and that she was going to help me out every step of the way, typing my letters and briefs, answering the phone for me. It was a pretty little speech, and I suppose the way she said it—all breathless from dancing—made everybody shout and clap some more. The orchestra began playing "Here Comes the Bride," and the people applauded us all the way back to our table. Before we sat down we waved and they clapped some more.

A few minutes later a tall, heavy-set man came over to our

table, "I'm Ed Fenimore," he said. He was holding a cone-shaped party hat in one hand, with his other hand over the top of it to keep the contents from spilling on the floor. On his finger he wore a big square-cut diamond that caught the lights from the dance floor and sparkled. The red and gold metallic paper hat glittered, and Sally's giant brown eyes were as bright and glistening as Mr. Fenimore's ring. For a moment I was conscious only of glittering. Everything seemed to shine, until Mr. Fenimore removed his hand from the top of the hat and revealed the folded and crumpled bills—tens, twenties, even fifties, stuffed up to the very brim of the hat. "It's for you," he said.

I took the hat and stared at it. "We can't take this," I said. "We're not professionals. We were just having fun."

"I know you were, son," he said. "Everybody in this room knows you were having fun. That's why we all chipped in. We want you to go on having fun."

Sally said nothing. She was looking at the money. I kept repeating, "But we can't take it—we were just dancing."

"Look," he said. "I know it's a struggle getting started. I've been in business myself. Take this—it'll help. Look at all the old fogies like me in this room. They're all rich. They've made their money. You're just starting out. The rest of them are too old to enjoy their money—you're not. It did their hearts good to see the two of you with your bright, young faces, out there, dancing—"

"But we never dreamed—" Sally whispered.

Mr. Fenimore pulled up a chair. "Mind if I sit down?" he asked. "Mind if I buy you a drink?"

"Oh, please sit down," Sally said.

"Let me buy *you* a drink," I said.

But Mr. Fenimore insisted. He flagged a waiter and gave him the order. Then he turned to Sally. "I hope you don't mind an old coot like me sitting down with you."

"But you're not an old coot," Sally said. "You're one of the sweetest men I've ever met. We're—well, we're just overwhelmed!" Her eyes kept returning to the money in the paper hat.

Mr. Fenimore told us a little about himself. He had retired and was a widower. He loved young people. He liked to see young people having a good time. He spent a lot of time in resorts, in hotels like this one. He traveled a great deal.

"I'm a resort bum," he said. "Nothing else to keep me busy."

But he was not like the other resort bums, he said, pointing around the room. For one thing, he was not so rich as they. Yes, he said, he had had money once. But he was spending it all. Soon, he said, laughing—he tapped the diamond ring—he'd have to sell that. Then he would be just a bum.

Being a resort bum was a lonely life, he said. There were seldom any young people in resorts like this, except an occasional honeymoon couple like Sally and myself. That was why we were so refreshing—like rays of sunshine.

"You kids are a couple of sweethearts," he said. "You brought back youth to everybody in this room. Take this money. It's worth it to them. If they can buy back five minutes of their youth with a pathetic ten or twenty bucks apiece, it's worth it."

Sally looked directly at him and smiled. "I guess we're just a couple of dancing fools!" she said. She leaned over and kissed Mr. Fenimore lightly on the cheek.

Now we are back upstairs in our room, and Sally has been counting and re-counting the money; there is more than $1,100. I would feel better if we could give it back, but Sally insists that we keep it. "This is more money than you'd make as a lawyer," she says. "Ed Fenimore is right. Those old fools don't need it, but we do!"

It disturbs me to hear her speak this way. It reminds me of the time, before we were married, when I gave a fellow some legal advice at a party. I gave him a hint about setting up a contract, and he called me up later to thank me. My advice had saved him some money. When I told Sally about it, she wanted me to send him a bill. I tried to explain that I couldn't —that I was still in school, that I didn't even have a degree. "Pretend you have a degree," she said. "You can have a phony letterhead printed. Why should he make money, and not you?"

Behind Sally's lovely face there is a mischievous streak, something a little daring and wanton. Perhaps that is why I love her so. I feel she needs me to control this in her. I must, by my example, help her to be less reckless, to think more of what is right.

I have agreed, however, to stay on at the hotel for a few more days.

Acapulco, January 30

All day I have been worried about keeping the money. It doesn't seem honest. But, Sally points out, there is nothing dishonest about it. She reminds me of what Mr. Fenimore said. She reminds me of how much we need the money. And now she has another plan.

Her plan sounds fantastic. And yet, she explains, it worked once. Why shouldn't it work again? And again and again? Why shouldn't every night bring us a thousand dollars, for a thousand and one nights, for as long as we wish? After all, there are hundreds, thousands of resort hotels like this one all over the world. Places where rich Americans gather to play, to be entertained, and to spend their money. A dance contest like the one last night is not an unusual thing. Aren't there other hotels—in Cuba, Nassau, Bermuda, France, Italy, Majorca—where the same thing would work?

For a while I didn't think she was serious. "Why don't we just set up a night-club act?" I asked her joshingly.

But, no, she explained patiently, that would not work. That was not it at all. Didn't I realize, exactly, what our assets were? We weren't sleek, polished professionals. Our assets were my boyish face, my crew cut, my fresh-out-of-college look, my Ivy League suits. Her assets were her impish face, her soft brown curls, her tiny waist and feet, her pretty backless cotton dresses, her fresh sun tan.

"We look well scrubbed," she said. "We're attractive, and we're *young,* don't you see?" She tried to find the exact word to describe us. "We're cute!" she said finally. "We look like somebody's son and daughter, like Joe Bowler drawings. We look innocent. The dancing we do is fresh and youthful and clean-cut. Don't you see?" she asked me. "That's the secret of our appeal. It's our charm!"

I asked her if she had always thought of us this way. It surprised me that she could analyze us so objectively. She said that it had just come to her today, when she was thinking about what Ed Fenimore had said. And, of course, her pretty little speech, holding the champagne bottle cradled in her arms like a baby, had been part of it, too, she said. So was her breathless, starry-eyed, deep-in-love look at me.

"Is that deep-in-love look something you can turn on and off whenever you want?" I asked her.

She laughed her small, tinkly laugh. "Of course!" she said.

I am opposed to the whole idea. But it is hard to refuse her. This evening, in the room, she has been rehearsing that little speech again and again. It must always sound spontaneous, she points out. It must always sound innocent.

I have agreed to try it just once. Tomorrow we are flying to Mexico City. We will try it there.

Mexico City, February 3

Last night it worked. We collected $800. It was a smaller room. Sally is beside herself with excitement. Today I have begged her not to make us try it again. I am sure that if it works again she will never let us stop. But she is obsessed with the idea. Tonight I looked at her, and suddenly I didn't know her. She was a different girl, a girl I'd never met.

Sally wants to try it once more. She feels—and I'm sure she's right—that we must not stay in Mexico. We are apt to be recognized. She is busy now with a travel book, figuring out where to go next. I feel that I should take a firm stand.

Palm Beach, Florida, February 9

We have done fairly well in Florida. We have covered two hotels, one in Miami and one here. Fourteen hundred dollars altogether. It seems incredible, but it is working. I have never seen Sally like this.

Sea Island, Georgia, February 27

The last three places have not been successes. Little things have been going wrong—intangible things that we can't explain. After each failure we have sat up at night trying to analyze it, trying to put our finger on the mistake. We are dealing in emotions, in moods. Sometimes we simply cannot seem to create the mood we need. Even the little speeches have been going wrong, although Sally has rehearsed and rehearsed. She has hit upon the idea of suggesting, very casually, to the social director or to the orchestra leader that a dance contest be held. But in the last place the orchestra leader refused. Was it because he was suspicious? And even when the leader agrees we're never sure that the hat will be passed. Last night the hat was passed, but we collected only a small amount, silver and a few dollar bills.

I had hoped that these failures would persuade Sally to let us give it up. But she is determined now to try the West Coast —California. Fortunately, we still have some money left.

Tahoe, California, March 3

Success again here last night. Five hundred dollars, which is really all we ever hope for in one night. Sally's plan is to go down the California coast—Santa Barbara, La Jolla, Caliente.

Santa Barbara, California, March 9

More bad luck today. Last night a newspaper reporter took a picture of us as Sally was making her speech. It is in this morning's paper. We are ruined now in this part of California. We must cancel La Jolla. Sally has mentioned a hotel in Las Vegas that is supposed to be very expensive, very rich. I am afraid there may be a Chicago crowd there that would recognize us but, as Sally points out, there is no way of knowing that until we get there. We will go and take our chances. I have persuaded her that there will be no more airplane travel for a while. We will go by bus. Funds are getting dangerously low.

Las Vegas, Nevada, March 12

Again a failure. I am convinced that our luck is running out. Our money is dwindling, and it frightens me to think of what will happen when it is gone. Sally wants to try Europe next, but it will take many good nights and bad nights. This morning we quarreled badly.

I begged Sally to let us stop, to let us go home.

"Just one more night," she insisted. "I'm sure we'll hit it the next place we go. There's a big hotel outside of Phoenix—let's try that."

I asked her to promise that, no matter what, the night in Phoenix would be the last.

She gave me a small, curious look. "And if I won't promise?" she answered.

I said I would go home without her.

She continued to look at me. "Very well," she said. "You can go home. I'm going on. Do you think you're the only man in the world who can dance with me? I'll find another partner. It won't be hard."

Sally was a poor girl. Perhaps that is the reason. She had no home, really. She had to work for everything she ever had. And now she is possessed by the promise of money. I can't leave her—I know that. But tonight I realize that in my own weakness I am bound to her forever—but not by love, as I had thought. Our hands and feet are bound together in dance steps, my arm about her waist.

Phoenix, Arizona, March 15

It began well last night. An elimination dance was started without Sally's suggestion, which is always a good sign. For then it all seems unplanned, spontaneous. The audience enjoys it more. There were perhaps 150 people in the room—women in minks and sables, men in dinner jackets. If it worked, I figured it might be seven or eight hundred dollars. The contest began, and soon, as usual, Sally and I were the only couple left on the floor.

The music quickened, as it always does when the orchestra catches our tempo and recognizes our skill. It was the most challenging moment of the evening, when the mood had to be right. I tried to do my best. But behind Sally's smiling, laughing eyes I could see what no one else could see, the dark shadow of fear. I realized we were dancing for our lives now. So much depended on the next few minutes. The next few minutes would tell us whether the audience would be ours, whether the applause would rise. If we succeeded, the future would be passed to us in a paper hat. If we failed, there would be no return. We would have to move on. "Now!" Sally's voice breathed the signal. And we began our fantastic twirls.

I suddenly wondered where we were spinning to, with the lights above us whirling like crazy stars. I felt we were on a merry-go-round far out beyond the limits of the night. Would we catch the brass ring? Perhaps, I thought, looking at her, if there was an answer, it lay hidden somewhere behind that impenetrable smile, in that look of fear. But, twirling her faster and faster, the answer eluded me again, as it has before. "Smile!" I heard her say.

With a burst, the music stopped. We stood, breathless and swaying, clinging to each other in the center of the floor. A spotlight fell upon us. Then the applause rose. It was going to be a good night. The prize—a purple orchid for Sally and a red carnation for me—was ready. The microphone was being moved toward us.

"I guess—I guess—" Sally began breathlessly. "I guess you'd call us a couple of dancing fools!" She laughed her little glittery laugh. She went on with her speech.

I looked out. Beyond the spotlight the room was dark. I could make out no faces. She came to the part about my going back to Evanston to practice law—how she wished we could stay on here, continue our honeymoon forever, it was so beautiful. But, alas, we had almost no money left. So we would be going home, and she would be helping me out, every step of the way. I already had my law books, she said—most of them. She was adding a little to the speech, but it was essentially the same. I could hear, in the darkness from the tables, the sound, the hushed voices, that told me that the hat was being passed. Sally squeezed my arm. We were both bowing, thanking them, smiling. The lights came up, and we headed toward our table. "Make this the last time," I whispered. It was then that I noticed a stout man in a white dinner jacket, heading toward us, pushing between the crowded tables, smiling curiously. For a moment I couldn't place the man's face. Then, with a kind of horror—I saw that it was Ed Fenimore. And I saw that his diamond ring was gone.

Montego Bay, Jamaica, April 22

Tomorrow we move on. There is a new place, a hotel in the Bahamas, that is supposed to be very fancy, very rich. Our reservations were confirmed this morning. After that we may try South America. We have decided that too long a stay in the West Indies would be dangerous; the news of us is beginning to spread. I don't know how long it will last. Sally says two more years, at least. Perhaps it will. Sometimes, when I remember all the dreams I had for us, I think my heart will break. The dreams I had for me, for Sally. It is hard to believe that the girl I married, and will live out my life with, could have brought us to this. Was I weak? It is too late now to ask.

Last night was very good. Nearly $1,000. It helps, as Sally knew it would, to have someone in the audience now, to start the hat around. We have worked things out so that Ed Fenimore stays in a different hotel from ours. That way no one suspects that we are traveling, as it were, together.

BLIGHTED CEDAR

✿✿✿✿ "Come on," he said.

The wide stretch of coral sand in front of the hotel led out in two directions—eastward, toward Hamilton, and to the southwest, around the point, toward the Cambridge beaches. There were a few stragglers left, but most of the swimmers had gone in from the beach to their Martinis and their thin toast sandwiches, and, a strait-laced few, in to the colorless interiors of the more conservative hotels for their tea.

The woman was wearing a peach-colored bathing suit and a broad straw hat. Over her suit she had tossed a bright yellow terry beach robe. The man was in knee-length shorts and a sweater. As they turned together—they had taken the eastward stretch of beach for their walk—and started back toward the hotel they scuffed their sneakered toes deeply and rebelliously into the sand, kicking it out in wide splashes at either side, leaving a broad crablike trail behind them. Their legs were caked with sand. Their faces had achieved almost exactly matching tans from the Bermuda sun, and from the cosmetic lotion that they both used, and if anyone had watched them from the distant terrace of the hotel they would have appeared as two small, brown, strutting birds.

"I *am* interested in your character," the woman said, "but I'm also interested in Barbara's future. Why can't you give me a direct answer to things?"

"What difference does it make what I say?" he said.

"I just want to make it final, that's all," she said. "Please, Frank, say yes or no."

He didn't answer her, but increased his pace, making her do a little two-step to catch up with him.

The beach was different now from the way Frank remembered it as being—in those wonderful prewar days. Then, he remembered, there had been many more children romping in the sand. There had been stately English nurses who sat erect in their private *chaises* and knitted while their eyes followed the children. There had been lifeguards in spanking white trunks, and the sudden dark contrast of colored boys who brought cocktails out to you on the beach. Now there was a different crowd, mostly Americans like Louise and himself. And the beach didn't seem to be kept as clean. Long, curved festoons of drying kelp gathered in rows, marking each foot or two of receding tide, and the beach boys seemed too busy to sweep them away. The line of shore behind the beach was different, too, with the blighted cedar trees standing gnarled and gray and graceless, leaving the white-roofed houses of the archipelago looking oddly startled and naked.

"It's for Barbara's own good, Frank. You've got to see that it is. We'll explain it to her tonight, after the birthday party."

"This place has gotten very ugly," he said. "I think I miss the cedar trees the most."

"Please, Frank," she said. "Will you please pay attention to me?"

"Let's hurry," he said.

"Wait," she said. "Now just stop here and wait a minute." She pulled his arm. "We've got to get this thing settled once and for all."

He stopped. "What do you want me to say?" he asked.

"Just say it's all right."

"For us to murder her child? All right. It's all right for us to murder her child."

"Frank, it's not murdering her child. It's saving her from disgrace. Which would you rather have?"

"There's no answer to that," he said. "How can I answer that?"

"You've got to. Listen. It's not as though Barbara were the first woman in the *world* to have this operation. Why, in many countries it's no more uncommon than a—than an appendicitis. And in Barbara's case—"

"In Barbara's case," he said, "I think we might discuss it with Barbara."

"Barbara knows."

"How does she know? You've never mentioned it."

"She knows. She suspects, anyway. Why does she think we brought her here?"

"And do you think she wants to handle it this way?"

"I don't see how Barbara can judge *what* she wants at this point," she said. "I think Barbara is—frightened, a little—at either of the alternatives."

"How can you be so analytical about it?" he asked her. "You talk as if Barbara weren't your daughter at all."

"I'm trying," she said, "simply trying to be common-sense. To do the sensible thing. A child has no right to live without a father. And how could we have the scandal of a lawsuit, or something, if we told him, and if he refused—if he wouldn't—"

Frank thought he detected a note of terror in her voice. "Don't you see? Don't you see how awful it could be?"

"I don't see how it could be awfuller than it is," he said. "Come on, let's get back."

"Then you do say yes?" she asked him, swinging into step beside him. "Is your answer yes?"

"Do what you want to, Louise."

"We'll explain the details to her after the birthday party," she said. "She'll be in a good mood then. Let her have a drink or two, Frank, to relax her. Then I'll phone Alexander and tell him where to bring the car. . . ."

"I'll dope her up, and then your strong-arm man can come out of the bushes, truss her up, and haul her off to that doctor. . . ."

"Frank, please don't talk like that."

She went on. "I'll run hot water in the bathtub. He wants her to be bathed before she gets there. He'll be awfully short of time."

"How will you lure her into the tub? Or will you push her in? Tell her it's for her own good, just a little birthday present—?"

"Oh, Frank, please! We're almost to Mrs. Redland's cottage. She'll hear you. Oh, hello there, darling," she called. "How are you?"

Mrs. Redland waved gaily from her stone-paved terrace—too gaily, Frank thought. It was as though Mrs. Redland waved out of habitual boredom.

"Coming to Barbara's birthday party?" Louise called.

"Wouldn't miss it for the world, Louise. See you then."

The two of them continued on, past the bare and straggly

row of trees that marked the actual boundary of the hotel's property. They walked more slowly now and Louise spoke softly and carefully.

"Her bag will have been packed. But I want you to bring it down to the car, at the east door."

"How much does this Alexander know about all this?"

"I have no idea. The doctor simply told me we could trust him."

"Why couldn't we take her there ourselves, in a taxi?"

"I think a private car is better, Frank. And so does he. He'll call us as soon as it's over. He doesn't expect any complications, since she's still in the early stages—"

He was out of her world, and the fact astonished him. He could hear everything that she said clearly and yet, somehow, it seemed as though none of it really involved him. Probably, he thought, it was because nothing he could say or do would stop her. In an hour or two friends would begin to gather for the birthday party. The wonderful joke was that it was Barbara's, Barbara's nineteenth birthday party. Soon a little private car would drive to the east door. Alexander would wait, fully instructed, trustworthy. Frank would see to it that Barbara had one or two drinks. Then it would be time for him to bring Barbara's suitcase down. Meanwhile Louise would be drawing water in the tub—fresh, soft Bermuda rainwater (did they really keep goldfish in those cisterns? he wondered). Downstairs Philip would be busy pouring champagne for the last of the guests, and finally, when she was a little tight, Barbara would be led upstairs and be told. Then down, out through the back elevator she would go, off for her abortion with her suitcase and the tiny silver good-luck spoon clipped in her hair, his own daughter. It was going to happen. He could never stop it, never. Alone, in their suite, he and Louise would wait for the telephone to ring. Louise would sit quiet, consuming cigarette after cigarette, and he, perhaps, would wait with the whiskey decanter.

They were at the foot of the wide white flagstone steps that led up to the hotel terrace from the beach. Louise stopped him again. "I think it would be nice, Frank, if we bought Barbara that little fur she admired in Bendel's window—when we get back, of course. Just a little something to prove to her that we still love her."

"Yes," he said.

"It wasn't terribly expensive. But if you feel you can't afford it right now, I can draw another check . . ."

"Yes," he said. "You could do that." Once upon a time, he thought, they had all been his checks, none of them Louise's. Perhaps, if they were still his checks, he could do something now, about Barbara. He turned and looked back across the beach. The tide seemed to be coming in now. He remembered the other years, watching Barbara on the beach, running to pull her back if she went too close to the surf, taking her by the hand. Barbara had trusted in him then. But now she was grown up. And he was betraying her.

"Do you like those cashmere skirts, Frank? I was thinking we might get Barbara one of those—with a little matching sweater. . . ."

"Yes, Louise. . . ."

"Oh, Frank," she said, "I know it bothers you to think about Barbara going to that doctor. But I assure you he's all right. And it's the only thing we can do, Frank."

"Yes, I suppose so."

"Then brighten up a little bit, Frank. At least *pretend* to. Or she'll certainly suspect—"

"Louise, what would happen if we called the boy and told him?"

"Oh, Frank—don't put obstacles in the way now. It's impossible, just impossible. He's in *college,* Frank—and he has no means of support. And his people have nothing, literally nothing. And of course she couldn't be in love with him."

"And if we let her—just *have* the baby?"

"It would ruin her life, that's all. No woman would want that. I know, Frank. I'm a woman. You've just got to accept that fact about women."

"You win, Louise," he said.

"After all," she continued, "it's really not such a dreadful thing. Two weeks' rest and she'll be as healthy as a horse. No one will ever know a thing. She can meet some *nice* young man—"

"Come on," he said. "I feel a little chilly."

They started up the steps. "Why, *there* you are, Frank Caldwell!" someone in heavy gold bangles exclaimed. "You promised me a game of tennis this afternoon, do you remember that? I saved a court for nearly an hour!"

Frank forced a smile. "I had to make some arrangements for the party," he said. "Will you be there, Molly?" The woman in the bangles nodded violently. "By the way," she said, "where *is* Barbara? I haven't seen her for hours."

"I think she's lying down right now," Frank said. "We'll see you at seven."

"There's a divine Princeton man I want her to meet—simply divine! If I weren't old enough to be his—his big sister, why, I'd be in love with him myself! Such *tennis!* And he's just

Barbara's type. I do hope they'll get together. He's interested in guns. Brrrr! And all sorts of things. But he's really quite nice and refined, a lovely boy."

"See you at seven," Frank said.

In the lobby Frank waited while Louise made some last-minute calls from the pay phone. He sat down in a green leather chair and watched the canaries flying around among the philodendron leaves. He could see Louise talking quietly and efficiently behind the glass doors.

In the suite on the fifth floor the telephone was ringing. But the girl who was lying stretched crosswise on the bed was paying no attention to it. It made no difference to her who it might be. She turned over on her back, and presently the ringing stopped. Her eyes were red from crying. She lifted her feet and looked at her shoes. They were not new, but they were her favorite pair, and she had put them on for a reason. A few minutes earlier she had tried to telephone someone, someone in New York. But the operator downstairs had told her that at Mrs. Caldwell's request no off-the-island calls were to be accepted from Suite 5-C. And so he would never know.

It was horrible, of course. But then, too, it was rather interesting, she thought, to be able to lie back this way and watch the plans whirling around her, while all the time no one supposed she knew that the plans were spinning out, revolving. Yes, she knew, she knew. She laughed suddenly, for suddenly it all seemed rather funny. She tried to imagine her mother's face if she should find out she knew, and if she found out that, after all, she didn't care. It was almost too much to think about.

She got up and lit a cigarette, still shaking with small sobs of laughter. At the window she tried to see New York again. If only she could see home again, she thought, just for a minute, that would be something. But here she was so far away. There was no one anywhere who could help her now. Instead of anything she knew, or wanted to know, she saw a cool, curving stretch of Bermuda beach that shone indelibly white in the fading sunlight and a clear stretch of sea that turned from green to murky blue at the horizon. There were a few late swimmers now, waving brown arms, making deep dashes into the green water—splash!—shouting hellos, waving goodbys. She turned away.

No, there was no one. Where was her father? She wondered. She had always waited for him to pull her out when the waves began lapping over her head. But this time he had not come. And she knew that her mother would be back soon, chattering gaily about the wonderful birthday party, looking at her with little veiled looks of distrust. So she had no time to lose. She went to the small writing desk, sat down, and picked up a pen and a sheet of hotel stationery. The crest was emblazoned with soaring breakers.

"My darling—" she began. She wrote a few more words.

Then automatically, as though indeed there were nothing else in the world to do, she stood up and walked into the tiny kitchenette. Feeling young and cheated and alone, she closed the door, fastened the window tight, and turned on the three gas jets.

Downstairs Frank waited for his wife. When she came out of the phone booth, she said, "I've just been trying to call the apartment to get Barbara to come down, but no one answers."

"Shall I go up?"

"No. She's probably just sulking. She's been behaving so *strangely*—"

"She's probably asleep," he said. "What did you want her for?"

"Well, I thought it would be a good idea if she put in an appearance down here. You heard what Molly just said. There's liable to be enough talk next week, so I thought that if we just sort of promenaded around . . ."

"Yes, I suppose so. I'll go up."

"Well, let's go into the bar for one old-fashioned first. I always need *one* drink before entertaining. Come on." She took his arm.

"Good afternoon, Mr. and Mrs. Caldwell," the bartender said as they entered. "Everything is ready for a wonderful party."

"That's very nice, Philip," Louise said. Frank followed her to her favorite window table.

Philip followed to take their order. "Doesn't the shore look beautiful right now?" Louise said. "In this sort of twilight? Look at it."

"Ah, but the cedar trees," Philip said. "They are gone now, nearly everywhere."

"Perhaps they will grow back."

"Two Scotch old-fashioneds," Frank said.

"Well, drink up," Louise said when they had been served. "We'll drink to better fortune, Frank."

But he had not really heard her, although he did lift his glass. He had discovered something, something about the place, about the people they were, the person he was, about the kelp-strewn pale-pink beach and the blighted cedar trees. It was not just the cedars that were blighted. It was himself, it was Louise. Somehow they had been struck from within by some cankerous disease. This was his discovery, and he waited for the words to come with which to explain it to Louise. Yes, they were blighted—but Barbara was not, not yet. He would stop it. He would not let it happen to Barbara. He would not let Louise go through with it. He would announce his decision to Louise, and he would go upstairs and explain it all to Barbara. And somehow—he didn't know how yet—they would work it out. He ordered another drink, and nursed it slowly, in silence, treasuring his thought.

"We'd better go," Louise said at last. "It's getting late."

And then he decided he would not tell Louise. He would first go and phone the boy in New York. He would talk to the boy as the boy's own father would. He stood up. "Excuse me a minute, Louise," he said. He started across the room.

He felt suddenly triumphant, as though through some ingenious devising of his own he was steering his family narrowly from the very brink of tragedy. He was so jubilant, in fact, that when the young manager rushed up to him at the door of the phone booth to whisper the dreadful news to him he had to ask him to repeat it, and then repeat it again.

The Partly Parted

DOROTHY, DOROTHY!

✿✿✿✿ Surprisingly, the movie had not been about Africa. Robert, who had gone expecting to see women unclothed from the waist upward, was disappointed. Miss Ungewitter, who had suggested that they go in the first place, felt she ought to apologize as she led the children out into the bright glare of the street. But in the transition from the cinema land of enchantment to the business day of Monaco she lost the urge to do this and suggested the ice-cream shop not so much as a compensation for the movie's obscurity but simply because the day was very hot and she herself was fond of French ices.

Not that they do me a bit of good, she thought, as she herded the children along in front of her down the crowded street. Miss Ungewitter was a large woman and was conscious of her amplitude, but rather than risk ruining her health with a diet at her age, which was past forty, she chose instead to play down her size by wearing simple loose-bosomed dresses of inconspicuous shades of gray and brown with long rather boxy skirts. She braided her fine brown hair into a neat bun at the back of her neck, never wore rouge, and always bought sensible Oxfords with leather-fringed flaps and low heels.

Robert was rubbing his eyes and blinking back tears. Harriet, who was twelve, noticed this and pointed triumphantly. "Look, he's crying!" she said. "He's crying because the movie was so sad and the lady died."

Robert began to explain that it wasn't grief but the sun, the suddenness of it, coming out into the street like that, that always made his eyes water. But Harriet, skipping along the street beside Miss Ungewitter, would have none of his excuses, and she taunted him, singsonging "Cry baby, cry baby," until Miss Ungewitter smacked her behind and told her to act her age and behave like a twelve-year-old young lady, not like a baby, in a public street of Europe.

As they entered the shop Robert was silent. Secretly he knew that Harriet was right. As the unfortunate heroine had tossed and turned in that huge bed at the end, Robert had felt her fever on his own brow and his lungs had ached with her suffering. The tears came still, whether he wanted them to or not.

When they were seated on three stools in a row—first Miss Ungewitter, mopping her steaming brow with the back of her pink hand, then Harriet, stiff and erect and formal, and then Robert on the last stool—Miss Ungewitter took her handkerchief out of her raffia purse and handed it to Robert.

"There was certainly enough dying," Miss Ungewitter said. "For a picture about doctors, there was certainly enough dying to it. I'm sorry it wasn't about Africa," she added, and then, when the young counterboy approached them, she said, "Three ice creams," articulating each word clearly and carefully, and pointing at the same time to the round paper containers under the counter. She was still timid when it came to using French.

Harriet was wearing the large dangling earrings of silver metal, fashioned to resemble grape leaves, that her mother had sent her from California. Her hair was long and dark and it hung damply about the collar of her cotton ready-to-wear, and when she tossed her head as she was doing now the earrings batted to and fro against her cheekbones. Miss Ungewitter, watching her, said she looked as though she were swatting flies, her hair like a horse's tail. Harriet ignored her and began talking in a loud throaty voice that was intended to be similar to Barbara Stanwyck's.

"I think it's really nauseating," she said, "the way the French people have no regard for proper illumination. What I mean is it's so de*press*ing. Though I thought that Paris was very well lighted, didn't you?"

"Well, I think that neon is worse," Miss Ungewitter said. "It sharpens one's features so, that kind of light."

"I mean it's so depressing," said Harriet.

"Look at that man!" Miss Ungewitter exclaimed. "He's painting our—no, he's not. For a minute I thought he was painting our picture."

"Isn't he quaint!" Harriet said. Then, talking about the movie, she said, "The people had such a problem in those days getting enough to eat and clothe themselves with. Even little children used to go without milk in those days, and mother's milk was put right out on counters and sold the way cow's milk is today."

"Harriet!" said Miss Ungewitter. "Such talk! Where did you hear that?"

"My mother *happens* to have told me that," Harriet said witheringly.

"Well, I don't think it's proper for a young lady to discuss things like that," said Miss Ungewitter. Save us, she thought. What kind of ideas had that mother of theirs filled these children's heads with? It was easy to see why Mr. Bartholomew wanted them with him as much as possible. She'd give anything to be able to confront that woman—just once, that would be enough. Just face her. She'd tell her a thing or two about bringing up children. Though Miss Ungewitter had never seen their mother, she already had a very good mental picture of Mrs. Bartholomew. Oh, beautiful probably, probably blonde, flashy blonde, wearing slacks all the time and big perching hats. Systematically she erased the image of Mrs. Bartholomew from her mind. "Does yours taste like apple?" she asked, sampling her ice cream.

"It's so nauseating, I really can't taste it," Harriet said.

"Well, mine has a cidery taste to it," Miss Ungewitter said. "It has a spicy, cidery taste. Try yours," she said to Robert, who was looking steadily at the plate in front of him with his elbows on the counter.

"No."

"There, go on. It's good. It tastes like raspberry. Eat those little chocolate pieces."

"It's nauseating," said Robert.

"Give it to your sister then," she said crisply. "And stop using that word."

"No, I want it."

"Well, eat it before it melts." Oh, good lord in Kansas, she thought, ye gods and little fishes, what next? Perhaps ignore him. She directed her attention to her own plate, eating steadily. She had been Head Children's Book Buyer for one of the largest department stores in Chicago and had thought she understood Child Psychology, but sometimes these two had her beat.

"Have you ever had a meeting like that?" Harriet asked her

suddenly. "A man, coming to you after years and years, after you've grown old, wanting you back? Oh, I thought that was beautiful, the way she opened that door and there he was a thousand years old . . ."

"Not yet," Miss Ungewitter said. "When I send them packing, they don't come back sniffing around my door."

"That's because you are a cruel person," Harriet said.

"I suppose I've been cruel to you!" Miss Ungewitter said indignantly. "I suppose I'm cruel when I take you to the movies and pay your way in with my own hard-earned cash, just for a treat."

"If you treated your lover like that, you were very cruel," Harriet said.

"Who said I had any lover?"

"What about that man you told me about? That man with the birthmark on his cheek?"

"Never mind about him," Miss Ungewitter said. "He's long gone and was no lover of mine to begin with. He was a beau, that's all."

There was not a particle of truth in it, she thought, not one iota. It was nothing but make-believe. In real life no romance was that secure. The fences a person broke were never that easily mended. And him reappearing the way he did, just like that, at her door, making everything oh so all right again by simply reappearing, coming back. Tap, tap. Who is it? It's me, me come back. And then into the house, into her arms, then picking her up, carrying her up the stairs to die—oh no, not like that where she came from, or any other place for that matter. Once you said good-by, there it was, they didn't come back. With your beauty mark on your cheek and your curly hair, she thought. She wished Harriet had not mentioned him. Now she would be dreaming about him again tonight. "It's good, isn't it?" she said to Robert.

"It's all right."

Suddenly Robert saw a Catherine wheel and wanted one. He wanted to light it from the terrace at night and signal to the ships from Alexandria. They would see it and think it was the light from Saint-Tropez and missteer their ships into the treacherous water beyond the beach. It was only four francs. Could he have it? Miss Ungewitter thought, Oh, lord, yes, all right, get it then, and she handed him a ten-franc note to pay for it. Robert hopped off the stool and ran across the shop to the opposite counter to buy it.

"He's spoiled," Harriet said. "Don't you think?" She leaned toward Miss Ungewitter and whispered conspiratorially. "Do you think he's maturing properly? In California, Mother told me that Father was spoiling him, and I know that Father thinks he isn't maturing properly, the way he *asks* for things. I don't think you should always let him get his own way like that."

"I don't *always* let him get his own way," Miss Ungewitter began, trying to remember what it was that she herself had been told about gratitude long ago. "Gratitude is a funny thing," she said, not remembering now just what the exact thing was.

"When that little boy of theirs died in the movie," Harriet said, "I couldn't help thinking what if it had been Robert. Dying before he reaches his maturity." And she added in a husky whisper, "I don't think he has very long to live anyway, you know."

Miss Ungewitter nearly jumped off her stool. "What?" she said. "What do you mean? He's the picture of health, growing out of his clothes!"

"I know," Harriet said mysteriously, "but I have a funny knowledge."

Miss Ungewitter snorted. "What knowledge?"

"I just know."

Miss Ungewitter picked up her purse nervously. "Are you through with your nonsense and ready to leave?" she asked. It was uncanny the way that child had of throwing you off balance. Funny knowledge indeed! And yet the way she said it, saying a thing like that in a voice that sounded straight from the tomb. "I suppose you're a fortuneteller," she said tartly. "You ought to go into business."

Robert was back, pressing the coins and the wad of fragile paper money into her hand. "Six francs," he said. "Ten take away four is six francs."

"Thank you, Robert," said Miss Ungewitter.

"You see?" said Harriet. "You thank him. He doesn't thank you. That's why he's such a brat."

Robert paid no attention to her. "Wait till the ships see this," he said.

"I don't think you should set it off from the terrace," Miss Ungewitter said.

"Why not?"

"Because some ship might see it."

"That's what I want, some ship to see it and get wrecked on the rocks."

"Well, I don't think that's very nice," Miss Ungewitter said. "All those men killed. You can set it off in the garden after supper."

"On Fourth of July we set one off on the boat and no ships came," Robert said.

"Yes, but that was different," Miss Ungewitter said. "And

besides, on the boat didn't the chief steward come and tell you to stop when you were doing that?"

"Daddy was doing it too. He told us we could."

"Well, that was one time when your daddy was wrong in that particular case," Miss Ungewitter said.

Harriet said, "If the mariners did wreck on our beach, we could take them in, couldn't we?"

"Yes," Robert said. "We could take them in and give them dinner and tell them stories and hear all about the Sahara Desert."

"Feed forty or fifty people? Don't be silly," Miss Ungewitter said. "Now that's the end of it. You'll set it off in the garden or not at all, and that's final."

"Never mind, Robert, we'll see what Daddy says," Harriet said.

"And never *you* mind about what Daddy says," said Miss Ungewitter sharply. "It's what I say, and I say no. That's that."

"It's your Catherine wheel, Robert," Harriet said. "You can do whatever you want with it."

"Oh, so it's his Catherine wheel, is it? Well, you seem to forget that it was my hard-earned cash that bought it for him," said Miss Ungewitter. "And it's me who'll take it away from him if he doesn't do as I say."

"Indian giver," said Harriet.

Miss Ungewitter signaled the counterboy impatiently. "Check!" she called. *"Billet! L'addition!"*

"I could feed them," Robert said, "and take them into my cave, and . . ."

"And we could help them fix their boat," Harriet said.

"When I say final I mean final," Miss Ungewitter said. "Harriet, who told you you could wear those earrings? Give them to me before we go out into the street."

"No!" Harriet shouted. "They're mine! Mummy bought them for me in California and I'm going to keep them. They're the latest creation from Hollywood."

"Hollywood! You'll go to Hollywood all right," said Miss Ungewitter, not knowing exactly what she meant. "Check! *L'addition!*"

"They look stupid," Robert said.

"Just because you're *ignorant!*" Harriet said. "You and her are both ignorant, Daddy said so."

"He did not!"

"Yes, he did. He said she was ignorant."

Miss Ungewitter was paying for the ice cream. "Come along," she said, after she counted her change. "You're both going to bed without your supper."

"I won't be bossed by a common servant!" said Harriet.

"Stay here then. Stay here. Come along, Robert."

Harriet seemed close to tears. "I will stay here and *rot!*"

She followed them though, and when they were in the street once more she looked hard at Robert. "You look pale," she said ominously. "There's blood all over your lips."

Miss Ungewitter spun around in the middle of flagging a taxi. "Blood!" she cried. *"Where?"*

"Oh—it's only ice cream," said Harriet. "I thought it was blood."

"It is blood," said Robert.

The taxi stopped and Harriet got quickly into the front seat beside the driver, and Robert and Miss Ungewitter got in the back. Miss Ungewitter lay back on the hard horsehair cushion.

The day was hot and sweltering. Would it never end? Turning her head slightly as the little car mounted the steep street toward the summit of a hill, she tried to see those pink villas, those waxen junipers and cypresses and knotted ghostlike trees all wind-bent from the southern gale. But, jolting and banging along the cobbles, there was a heavy ground haze over everything and, between the yellow stucco buildings, the gray glint of the Mediterranean lying shrouded in fog, stirring restlessly under the great heat of it all.

Pillars of smoke rose straight from several chimneys, and there was a dark, foul smell in the air like the between-cars smell of trains, and the upholstery of the taxi itself exhaled a dead stench like faded lilies. There were no birds, no gnarled fingers of trees, nothing of the picture-book Azure Coast as she saw it, bouncing along with Robert's elbow jabbing hard into her thigh and Harriet's stiff back in front of her. Tricklets of perspiration swam down the hollow of her back. You curly-headed fool, she thought, would you come to France too? Scoundrel, scourge of my life. Behind the bushes, around the next corner of that wall she would see him lurking, wrinkling up his nose to smile at her. But he wasn't there, he had tricked her again. Oh, come back again, she thought.

"Do you think I'll ever get married?" Robert asked.

"Oh, I've no doubt you will someday," she said.

"When I do, I want to marry somebody like that Leona." His elbow dug sharply into her side and she reached down, pressing him gently away.

"Leona? Who is she now?"

"That lady with the Indians there."

"Oh, yes," she said, still not understanding. "The Indians."

"If she called like that, I'd get there before they did."

"Where? Get where?" They were nearly home now, round-ing the last corner. Appear now or forever hold your peace, she told him. Ahead was the gate and the driveway.

"To the fire, where they were going to burn her."

"Oh, yes," she said, remembering the movie. "Those were Spaniards though, not Indians."

"Harriet is ugly, isn't she?"

"No, Harriet is very beautiful."

"I don't think so," said Robert.

"Nobody cares what you think," said Harriet without turning around.

"Children, children!" said Miss Ungewitter. "We're almost home."

The taxi stopped and Harriet got out and started haughtily up the walk to the house. Miss Ungewitter counted out the money carefully, paid the driver, and gave him the usual tip. As the taxi drove away in the dust, she and Robert walked up the path together. Robert was clutching his parcel under his arm, and Miss Ungewitter took hold of his other hand. "You can set it off from the terrace if you like," she told him. If some captain was silly enough to mistake a child's firework for Saint-Tropez light, he deserved to wreck, she decided.

"I don't mind setting it off in the garden," Robert said.

"That's my good boy," said Miss Ungewitter. "Whatever you want to do."

The children's father didn't show up for dinner, but Miss Ungewitter had put on her good blue dress anyway, thinking that he might. And it was a good thing she had, because after the children had finished eating and she was sitting alone at the table with her coffee, he did come in. He was very sunburned.

"Good evening, Miss Ungewitter," he said. "How did it go?"

"Well, we went to a movie this afternoon, Mr. Bartholomew," she told him.

"Oh, remind me of that when I give you your check on Friday," he said.

"I don't mind, sir. I don't mind giving them a little treat."

"Were they good? Did they behave?"

"Good as gold," she said. "Oh, that Robert! He has a firework I bought him that he'll be setting off as soon as it gets dark."

"You shouldn't spend so much of your own money on them, Miss Ungewitter," he said. "You're much too generous, I've reminded you of that."

"Oh, it's my pleasure, Mr. Bartholomew," she said.

"I'm going over to the Casino with the Conrads," he said. "I'll probably be back before eleven, though."

"Have you had your dinner, Mr. Bartholomew?"

"Yes, I had dinner at the Conrads'. This was their dinner party, did I forget to tell you? I'll say good night to the children now."

"Have a good time."

"Thank you, Miss Ungewitter. Good night."

After he had gone Miss Ungewitter took her full coffee cup out onto the high terrace. The large tree in the center was full of enormous green blooms that were faintly malodorous, but the sun was going down and a cool breeze had come up almost chilly from the west. The hot sirocco from Robert's desert, she thought of it, cooled by its journey across the sea. It fanned and cooled her moist cheeks and forehead. The terrace frightened her so. It was a jumping-off place between here and the hereafter, this high, wind-swept patio with the hill falling away beneath it, and on one side the city was sprinkled like a crazy quilt at her very feet, and on the other side was the rocky beach with the waves breaking on it now. Coming in, coming in. Waves always came in, never flowed out. Timidly she walked to the very edge, then retreated several steps quickly. The children were safe in the garden behind the house. No one was aware of her peril. Distantly the telephone rang and distant feet pattered to answer it. Distant voices jabbered incomprehensible foreign words. The waves crashed far below. "Dorothy, Dorothy!" What? What is it? She almost spoke aloud.

The lights were turned on in the living room. Miss Ungewitter crossed the terrace and sat down heavily in one of the white peacock chairs and tried to remember where she had left her sweater.

Suddenly she saw Robert standing behind the trunk of the tree, watching her. "How long have you been there?" she asked him almost crossly, wondering whether she had been talking to herself.

"I'm waiting for it to get dark enough," he said.

"Where's your sister?"

"I don't know. In the house."

"Doesn't she want to watch while we set it off?"

"She says you're a fat old witch."

"Does she?"

"Are you?"

"Well, what do you think?"

"I don't know."

"Well, that wasn't a very nice thing for her to say, was it?" And she almost added "after I took her to a movie and bought her ice cream," but she thought better of it and said nothing.

"You are fat."

"I have a lot of height on me, don't forget," she said, "to make up for it. And I used to be quite slim, what's more."

"I don't mind if you're fat," he said.

"Come out of the shadows where I can see what I'm talking to," she told him. He stepped out. He was carrying the Catherine wheel. "I think it's dark enough," Miss Ungewitter said suddenly. "Here, I've got some matches. Let's set it off! Bring it over here."

"Nobody will see it," he said.

"Oh, yes, they will. All over town they'll see it. Ships at sea will see it, wait and see."

"But not Harriet or Daddy."

"Harriet is—" She wondered how to put it so that he would understand. Harriet—odd, gawky, cross Harriet, Harriet whose moods changed so fast you couldn't tell from one minute to the next *how* she would be, faster than you could say Jack Robinson. Harriet, who one minute wanted to love everybody and the next minute wanted to kill everybody and see them all lying dead at her feet. Harriet, who just that morning had asked what she could do about her front, it was growing so large, larger than any other part of her. Harriet who thought she was all out of proportion and who pretended to be a beauty queen to make up for it! "Harriet is too old," she said finally.

"She makes me sick."

"I know. Well, we must try to please Harriet sometimes." Miss Ungewitter stood up and smoothed the front of her blue dress with her fingertips. She took the Catherine wheel from him now. Suddenly, as she held it gingerly between her two forefingers, it took on the aspect of a deadly, dangerous weapon. Unlighted, it was calm and harmless, but touched with a match it was a spinning wheel of fire, the devil's own lamp.

Carefully she set it on the high wall of the terrace. Then she realized that it had to be nailed to something or it would simply spin itself over the edge. She looked around for a proper place for it. There was a spike in one of the branches of the tree where a swing had once been, and Miss Ungewitter pushed her chair to this spot and stepped up on the wicker seat to reach. The wind whipped her skirts tight against her legs. She fastened the pinwheel firmly to the spike and then lit several matches which the wind quickly blew out. Finally she had one going and she held it to the fuse, and then, seeing it was lit and sputtering, she jumped clumsily off the chair and grabbed Robert's hand. "Watch out!" she cried irrationally as the thing began to spin.

It spun at first slowly, lazily, and then, gathering momentum, it spun rapidly, wildly, with a great whirring sound, showering the leaves of the tree with sparks, lighting up the topmost branches, pricking out the ponderous blooms with shafts of red streaked with orange, and blue streaked with red fire, and in the center the light was blinding white like burning magnesium, and faster and faster it spun, and the sparks came huge now, great clusters of stars falling apart around that moon of light, and the sparks flew into the hollyhocks and over the edge of the terrace, down, down into the endless darkness.

Robert screamed with delight. The Catherine wheel spun on while everything stopped for Miss Ungewitter and the universe centered on this mad shining thing that powered itself and drew its deadly energy from some invisible sun. Robert was looking for shipwrecks now, and the wheel spun slower, slower, and the sparks were fewer, till finally, with a sputter of blue and gold and crimson, the wheel stopped, stood motionless, glowing for an instant, and went out.

It was a moment or two before Miss Ungewitter could say a word. "Harriet! Harr-i-*et!*" Robert was shouting. "Did you see it? Did you see it?"

Miss Ungewitter turned around and looked toward the house and saw that Harriet had, indeed, seen it. Harriet's face was pressed against the living-room windowpane.

"Tell me about it, tell me about it," Robert repeated, jumping and tugging at her hand. "What made it *do* that? Why did it keep going and *going?* Do you think a ship saw it? Do you think they saw it from the Casino?"

"I think the man in the moon saw it," said Miss Ungewitter. But what she couldn't tell him, what she herself even did not understand, was that for a moment—oh, only an untraceable moment in it—she had seen something, something in the burning center of that blinding sun, features etched in the white brilliance, features which assembled, materialized, and became for a moment two almost real eyes over a wrinkled nose above a smiling mouth that curled up and drew a sudden deep cleft in the birthmark on that cheek, his cheek, the last touch of reality. And for a moment there she had almost said, "Oh, you are here, you did come to France after all, you silly man, you did appear again." But then it had begun to fade.

"It's your bedtime," Miss Ungewitter said. "Harriet saw it—there she is, see her? She saw it. Come on, time for bed."

"Will you carry me?" he asked her.

"Oh, we're too old for that, aren't we? Going on seven? Well, maybe once more." He said that she couldn't, but she said, oh, yes, she bet she could, and to show him she could she picked him up by the armpits and for a couple of steps did carry him. Then she remembered Harriet still watching, and she thought, No more foolishness, enough is enough. He didn't mind, and did as he was told, walked like a man beside her into the house.

LYDIA

✿✿✿✿ The girl who was lying face down on the terrace beside the pool turned her face to one side and looked at the young man who was sprawled, or rather spread-eagled, on the yellow towel next to her. Her look was not one of invitation, nor was it one of rebuke. It was a practiced look, involving a slight arching of the eyebrows, a small upturning of the mouth, and a widening of the eyes. "What will you do if I tell you?" she asked. It was a flirtatious look; she was aware of it.

"Just call you by it," he said.

"Very well. It's Lydia," she said.

"Hello." She turned away from him and looked straight ahead, toward the pool and the swimmers, her chin resting on her folded hands. Directly in front of her, in a little arrangement, were a bottle of suntan oil, a raffia purse, a pack of cigarettes, a small enameled lighter, and a fashion magazine spread open, face down. She reached now for the cigarettes, extracted one carefully from the pack, and seemed to wait, still looking directly ahead, at nothing. The young man pulled himself up on his knees, reached for the tiny lighter and flipped it open, holding the flame in front of her.

She took her time noticing this. Then, cupping her hand

around his, she held the light he offered close to her cigarette, and inhaled. She let her eyelids flutter up now, to meet his eyes. Then she exhaled a sharp stream of cigarette smoke and continued looking straight ahead. The young man, who was blond, slim, and muscular (a lifeguard? she wondered), returned to his original position on the towel. Smoking, the girl said nothing.

She was twenty-nine, but could have passed, perhaps, for twenty-three or twenty-four. That is, she hoped so. She was slender, and her skin was very smooth. She was evenly and flawlessly tanned from two weeks of lying, first on her stomach, then on her back, in the Las Vegas sun. Her hair was light brown but the sun, aided by a chemical preparation, had bleached it to a reddish-streaked blonde. A stickler for perfection of detail in women's faces might have found her nose a little too small and her mouth a little too wide, but would have quarreled with little else. She knew how to use her face, how to compose it in a brooding, sulky look. Her mouth seemed to pout as she smoked. Her face had a finality, a definiteness that made men turn to look at her.

"Been here long?" the young man asked her.

"Two weeks," she said, not looking at him.

"For the usual reason?"

She looked at him now. "What usual reason?"

"For a divorce?"

She gave him her inviting-rebuking look again. "My, aren't we curious!" she said. She looked at him a moment longer, then looked away. It was not the perfect reply, she knew. What had been called for was some witty, some offhand and less mocking remark. But people frequently caught her off guard. Something was said that called for an amusing or sophisticated reply, and inevitably the thing she chose to say emerged sounding not amusing, but silly. Not sophisticated, but surly. She tried to make it a point to answer such remarks only with silence, but often she forgot. The trouble was—and she was aware of this just as she was aware of everything else about herself—that she was not clever or even particularly bright. It was the single flaw in an otherwise perfectly concocted human being. Being reminded of this made her expression even more petulant, and she started wishing that the young man would go away, handsome though he definitely was. Rising and falling moods were another problem. Trying to make her voice sound gay, she said, "Where are you from?"

"Nowhere in particular," he said.

"Nowhere? You must be from somewhere."

"Well, I'm from L.A. And I'm from here, too. Lots of places."

"Do you work here at the hotel?"

"No," the young man answered.

"What are you doing here, then?"

"I come here to swim."

She smiled. "Why here?"

"More pretty girls lie on this terrace than any other," he said.

There it was again: a remark that called for a bright, or at least an adroit, reply. And once again her mind was empty, like a television screen gone suddenly dead with no images or words. And while she groped, mentally, for dials that would produce sounds and meanings, the light, or whatever it was, in her head receded and drew in until it was only the smallest, almost invisible, white dot. She looked up at the sun, and then, walking toward her along the edge of the pool, threading his way between seated, reclining, and standing figures, she saw her salvation coming: Mr. Whatsisname, the man she had met the night before.

"Well, hello!" she said.

The man stopped and looked down at her. His expression was puzzled, almost startled. Then, recognizing her, he smiled. "Hi," he said. "How're you today?" His voice had a pleasant drawl.

"Just wonderful!"

"It's—ah—Lydia, isn't it?"

"That's right. How cute of you to remember!"

"How could I forget?" he said, smiling.

"Well," she said, "I've got a confession to make. I've forgotten your name."

"Sid Thurman."

"Oh, of course!" She paused. Then she said, "How are you feeling today?"

"Pretty good, pretty good," he said. "All things considered."

The girl laughed. "Well, we both certainly were *not* having our lucky day, were we? I haven't *dared* figure out how much I lost!"

"No more roulette for me," he said. "Craps. That's safer." He stood over her for a moment, smiling down. "Well," he said finally, "perhaps I'll see you again. Good-by."

"Good-by," she said. She lay watching him walk away, toward the far end of the pool, a graying, heavy-set man in blue shantung trousers and a vivid orange sports shirt.

The blond young man, who had been lying with his face buried in a well created by his arms, as if asleep, looked up now. "Well, well," he said.

"What do you mean, 'well, well'?" she asked.

"Sid Thurman."

"Well? Who's he?"

"Are you kidding?"

She looked at him. "No, who is he?"

"Just one of the richest men in Las Vegas."

The girl appeared suddenly interested. "Is that so?" she asked. "Really?"

"Sure. He's got oil wells pumping all over Fort Worth."

"Really? What's he doing here?"

"He lives here part of the time. Not here at this hotel, but he's got a house down the road. Spends a couple of months here every year."

"Well, for heaven's sake." The girl sat up suddenly and tucked her legs underneath her, tailor-fashion. "He never gave the impression—you know—of being wealthy. Of course he did lose a lot of money at roulette. I was with him last night. Not *with* him, really, but—you know—we were sort of standing together, in the casino. He lost—oh, I don't know how much. Maybe three hundred dollars." She laughed. "I should have guessed it. When he lost that much money, I mean, he didn't seem to care. Just sort of laughed it off!" She laughed again, tossing her head back. "Well, well! Isn't that interesting? I thought he was awfully nice. He bought me five stingers. Ooooh, what a head I had this morning!"

The young man looked up at her and grinned broadly. "Five stingers," he said. "That's a lot."

"I hardly ever, barely drink," the girl said. "I'm just not used to it."

"Ah," he said, "I bet you're used to it."

"I'm not," she said sharply, her face turning to a pout. "No, I'm not used to it." She looked away from him once more. From this seated position she could see farther. She could see across the pool, over the tops of pink and white umbrellas, over the red-tiled roof of the low, sprawling hotel, to a single, fat, absolutely motionless palm tree that seemed to shimmer, almost to steam, in the hot, still desert air. Studying its leaden, drooping green leaves, she felt her own spirits sink leadenly also, her morale drooping like the leaves. She remembered her hangover this morning, traces of which still persisted; she remembered the arduous, elaborate steps it had taken for her to rise from the bed, to open her eyes before the mirror. She had taken the B-1 capsules, but they hadn't seemed to help. Recovering from a hangover was getting to be more of a job. It required first those shaky, painful steps toward the bathroom; then acknowledging her face in the mirror, greeting it, as it were, to assure herself that the face, the girl, was still there. Then it took a long shower, first hot, then cold. Then room service for coffee, then aspirin, then more coffee. And then, though it tasted wretched, a cigarette. Then dressing, then fixing hair, face, putting on lipstick. Then a trip to the pool, a brief, cold immersion in the water and an hour in the sun. Then, finally, normality returned, and confidence, which was always helped by the arrival of a slim, handsome, blond young man, standing there holding his yellow towel and saying, "Can I spread out here?" In the two weeks she had been at Las Vegas, the mornings had been getting worse, not better. She didn't understand it. She had always, or so she thought, been able to hold her liquor, to drink with the best of them. But something had changed. Perhaps she was drinking more, or perhaps it was the boredom, the emptiness and bleakness of each day as it dawned, stretching dismally ahead of her. Like a prisoner, she had begun to tick off the days until she could go, until she would have her divorce. Until she would be free. Even the word "free" was beginning to lose its meaning for her. Free of what? Free of Tom. But even Tom was hard for her to think of now, and so being free of him—free of someone who already seemed to have vanished, to have diminished like the receding image on the television screen—seemed meaningless. They had been married for four and a half years. "I guess we both just had the four-and-a-half year itch," she had said to friends laughingly. The words, their marriage, the four and a half quarrelsome, confused years —nothing, actually, seemed to have any pertinence to her as she sat beside the pool. And she felt herself sinking into a great, deep chasm of despair. "What time is it?" she asked.

The young man looked at his watch. "Eleven-ten," he said.

"I'd better go," she said. She began picking up her things.

"Perhaps I'll see you around," the young man said.

"Maybe." She gathered her things and stood up. "Good-by," she said.

"So long, Lydia."

Walking back toward the hotel she realized that she did not even know his name.

She stopped at the desk. "Are there any messages for me?" she asked.

The room clerk consulted the row of mailboxes. "No, Mrs. Emerson," he said. And then he said, "Oh, yes—I forgot. Mrs. Morris says she can see you at eleven-thirty."

"Oh," Lydia said. "Thank you." She walked down the hall to her room and let herself in with the key. The room was dark, with the slats on the Venetian blinds tilted upward. She turned on the overhead light. She had forgotten, too, about the plans she had made yesterday morning, about seeing Mrs. Morris. And remembering this made her remember the diminishing sheaf of traveler's checks folded in the pocket of her suitcase.

She knew how many checks were left; she would not count them again. If she did, she would only feel bluer. She stood, irresolute, in the middle of the room. Then she went to her closet, opened the door, and studied what she saw there. She decided on a simple, yellow cotton sundress, which she could wear with the yellow shoes.

By eleven-thirty she was dressed and ready. She left the room and walked back down the corridor to the door marked MANAGER. She knocked on it.

"Come in," a woman's voice called.

Lydia opened the door. "Mrs. Morris?" she asked politely.

"That's right."

"I'm Mrs. Emerson."

"Come on in." The other woman stood up. Mrs. Morris was a large woman, perhaps forty-five, with silver-blonde hair that was arranged carefully all around her head like soft wax. She was wearing black slacks and a bright red silk blouse. Silver bracelets dangled heavily from both her wrists and she was smoking a crimson-tipped cigarette. "Sit down, honey," Mrs. Morris said.

Lydia sat down gingerly on the chair in front of the desk.

"What can I do for you?" the other woman asked.

Lydia cleared her throat politely. "Well," she began, "I'm sort of at loose ends here—getting my divorce and all. And I thought—well, I thought I really have nothing to do with myself all day—and I thought just *possibly* there might be something I could do here at the hotel."

The other woman stared at her. "In other words," she said, "you're looking for a job."

"Well—yes," Lydia said.

"What can you do?"

"Well—" Lydia began.

"Never mind," the other woman said, interrupting her with a wave of her hand. "I know. You can type. You can be a receptionist. Look," she said, "I don't need typists, I don't need receptionists."

"Well—" Lydia tried to speak again.

"Listen, honey," the other woman said, "level with me. What's happened? Are you broke? Can't you pay your bill?"

Lydia sat up straight. "It's not that—"

"What's the matter with junior? Your husband? Won't he send you any dough?"

"Now just a minute," Lydia said. "You don't seem to understand—"

"Just a minute yourself!" the other woman said. "Listen to me, honey. There's a million like you. They come in here every day. So don't give me that sweet and innocent 'I-thought-I-could-help-out' stuff!"

Lydia stood up abruptly. "I'm sorry," she said. "Thank you very much."

"Sit down!" the woman bellowed.

Lydia felt the tears coming. "No!" she said. "I won't be spoken to that way! I'm a guest here and—"

"Sit down." And suddenly the other woman's voice became sugary and cajoling. "Look, honey," she said, "I didn't say we couldn't talk, did I?"

"Obviously you have nothing for me," Lydia said.

"I said," the other woman said slowly, "that I didn't need typists and I didn't need receptionists. That's all I said, honey, so don't go flying off the handle."

"Well, what do you need?"

Mrs. Morris turned in her swivel chair and looked at the opposite wall. "I saw you with Sid Thurman last night."

"Yes, I was with him—" Lydia said.

"Look," the other woman said, "you're better-looking than most. You've got a little class. Thurman seemed to think you were okay. I could use you—" and she punctuated the sentence with a long pull on her cigarette— "I could use you in the casino. As a hostess. Six nights a week. A hundred dollars a week."

"That's not what I had in mind," Lydia said.

The woman turned sharply on her. "Sure it's not!" she said savagely. "But it's all you're going to get from me! So think it over. Let me know."

"I—" Lydia began. But she couldn't finish. She turned and ran out of the office and down the corridor to her room. She let herself in, then locked the door from the inside. She turned, striking her thigh hard on the protruding metal arm of a chair, and threw herself across the bed, sobbing—sobbing both from the pain of the bruise and from humiliation.

At twelve-thirty she was still lying on the bed, still softly sobbing. Then she stopped sobbing and didn't move.

There followed a series of images, some sharp, some blurred and fantastic, on her mind that seemed to resemble a television screen. She saw Tom once, clearly, in the living room of their house outside Chicago. His face, in this vision, was twisted with rage. He was calling her unkind, unforgivable things, things she couldn't hear and couldn't answer. He had never understood her. He was angry, this time about Barry, Barry Whosis, that man at the country club, and it was so ridiculous of him to be angry about a man whose name she couldn't even remember, who had made no more impression upon her than that. He didn't understand that it was just a harmless flirtation; he didn't understand that harmless flirtations were one of the few pleasures of her life. She remembered the flirtations, the faceless, forgotten men, all with names that sounded like Barry. Barry, Larry, Harry.

Tom could be sweet, but he could be cruel, too, and that night his bitter words made her run out of the house and into the car. She saw herself driving to Sally Campbell's apartment. Sally was her best, her only, and her dearest woman friend. Sally was divorced. "You poor kid," she heard Sally say comfortingly. "Tom is a rat. I always thought so." And Sally mixed her a good, stiff drink and for hours, it seemed, the two of them had sat numbly and joyfully counting off the weaknesses and shortcomings of all men. "Get the car. Get the house. Get a third of his salary at *least,*" she heard Sally's flat voice saying. "Get the war bonds . . . get the cash . . . get the furniture." Then that whole vision was interrupted with a young man's pleasant voice—how young was he?—saying, "Can I spread out here?" And the joy of looking up and saying to yourself: My, he's good-looking. And the joy of smiling, arranging the face in the smile that was not too inviting, not too unfriendly either, the upward look of the eyes, the arch reply, "All right." And the blissful, dumb, numb feeling of knowing about yourself: *You look good to him; he likes you.* And then across this pleasant picture, like an obtrusive commercial, came the figure: $480 in traveler's checks. Seventeen dollars in my purse. And the dismal wondering, Can I get any more from him at this point? Before I get the decree? Just two weeks before, Tom had written out the check—grimly—for a thousand dollars. It would have to be enough, he had said. He was paying the attorney's fees as well. Where had all that money gone? How had she run through more than half of it in two weeks? The room wasn't expensive! She knew the answer, of course. It had gone, evaporated in the casino and in the bar. She had been a fool to try the gambling tables. How much had she lost last night? Probably fifty or sixty dollars; she couldn't think.

Then that picture, too, dissolved. And clearheadedly she thought, Things aren't so bad! Mrs. Morris offered me a job, didn't she? Maybe it wasn't exactly—precisely—what she'd had in mind. At first thought, it didn't seem dignified. It seemed sort of degrading—being a hostess in the casino. But, after all, what was wrong with it? Really nothing. A hundred dollars a week—that would tide her over. But then she thought, No. It was degrading. She couldn't bring herself to do it. What if there should be someone from home, who should come in, see her there? She could never live it down. Tom had made good money as a regional sales manager. She had always had nice things. He had called her dumb, he had said she had no education, which wasn't true because she had gone to secretarial school. And he had called her cheap because she came from the South Side. But she had come from a respectable home, as good as Tom's, and she had been brought up to be a lady. He had made good money, she had always had nice things; she had always held her head up and Tom had been proud of the way she looked and dressed. So she wouldn't stoop to that. Not, anyway, except as a last resort. And then, in this dream of money, ease and lovely things, nice clothes and the way she liked best of all to live, she thought of Mr. Sid Thurman. She, Lydia Emerson, had actually been found attractive by one of the richest men in Las Vegas! How interesting! How green with envy Sally Campbell would be! She saw herself—was it so impossible?—

as Mrs. Sid Thurman of Fort Worth, Texas! And with this thought—though perhaps these thoughts were sleeping-dreams already and not waking ones—she fell asleep.

She didn't wake up till four. And, waking, she felt new life and determination seeping into her. She sat up and reached for the telephone. "I would like," she said, "to place a long-distance call—collect—to Evanston, Illinois." And she gave the operator the number and her name.

A minute or two later she heard Tom's voice say, "Hello?"

"Tom?" she asked hesitantly.

"Yes."

"It's me, Lydia, Tom," she said.

"Yes. So the operator said," he replied.

Again, it was the disconcerting remark. The remark she hadn't expected, coming abruptly, throwing her off guard. But she began talking rapidly anyway. "Tom," she said shrilly, "this is Lydia, Tom. Tom, I'm terribly afraid I need more money— don't interrupt, Tom! Tom, you just didn't give me enough. A thousand dollars isn't going to be enough; I'm sorry but I'll need a thousand dollars more, Tom, right away. No, no!" she cried, although he had said nothing. "No! I won't listen to any more of your remarks! Listen here. I can get it this way or have your salary attached, my lawyer says so, Tom, he said that I could ask you decently to do the proper thing or else—" She was lying wildly now. "Or else, you listen to me, Tom, or else I'll attach your salary and that would be pretty embarrassing for you with Mr. Wilson at the office, wouldn't it?" She said several more words before she realized—how could he!—that the connection was dead; he had hung up on her.

At six o'clock—the desert sky was darkening and she had turned on her bedside lamp—she called Sid Thurman. Another man, a butler probably, answered the phone. There was some delay before she heard Mr. Thurman's slow Texas drawl.

"Hi, there!" she said brightly. "It's me—Lydia Emerson."

"Lydia?"

"Yes—from last night. And this morning by the pool. Remember?"

"Oh, sure," he said. "Sure, I remember. How are you, Lydia?"

"Fine," she said. "Just fine."

"Swell," he said.

"Say," she said, "I'm wondering if you'd like to buy a girl a drink tonight?"

"Tonight?"

"Yes," she laughed, "I'm rested, showered, all dressed up and no place to go!"

"Gosh, Lydia," he said, "I can't do it tonight. My—well, my wife is sick."

She paused, but only for the barest second. "Oh," she said. "Oh."

"I'm really sorry, Lydia."

"That's all right," she said dully.

"If my wife weren't sick—"

"Of course," she said. "I understand."

She replaced the receiver on its cradle.

Then it was not until seven o'clock, when the sky was full of sunset and shadows, that she was ready to leave her room. She had spent a long time in front of the mirror, repairing the ravages of the day. The eyes, especially, needed work. By outlining the lids with pencil, deepening them with blue eyeshadow, and adding mascara, she had managed to erase most of the effects of crying. Then she experimented with her hair in a new way, pulling it back, away from her face, little-girl fashion. She wondered, briefly, how it would look dyed golden red. Not bad, she decided. She had put on the pale-blue backless cocktail dress with the sequined top and fastened pearl earrings to her ears. She assembled things for her purse—lipstick, cigarettes, the lighter; she tore two twenty-dollar traveler's checks from the packet in her suitcase and placed them, loose, in with the other things. That would be her limit. She would try the tables one more time.

She walked out of the room, locking the door behind her, went past the reception desk, out onto the terrace by the pool. The underwater lights had been lighted in the pool, and from the dining room and cocktail lounge on one side dance music floated. On the other side was the casino, already beginning to sound gay. At the far end of the pool, tables were set up for cocktails.

Lydia looked at it all for a moment or two, and then she saw the tall, blond young man approaching. He was no longer in bathing trunks, but in a plaid Madras jacket, and he looked even straighter and more handsome.

"Hello," he said, and smiled at her.

"Hello," Lydia said.

"Got a date tonight?"

"No, as a matter of fact I haven't."

They started walking around the lighted pool.

"You know something?" she said. "I don't know your name."

"Don," he said.

"Just Don?"

"Just Don. You're just Lydia, aren't you?"

She laughed softly. "Yes, I'm just Lydia."

They walked in silence. Then he said, "I figured you might be out with Sid Thurman tonight."

"Sid Thurman," she said firmly, "had just better take care of his wife."

"His wife?"

"Yes, his wife is sick."

The young man stopped. "Is that what he told you?" he asked.

"Yes. Why?"

"Ah, you poor kid," he said.

"What do you mean?"

"Sid Thurman doesn't have a wife."

"What!" Without her wanting it to, the word came out as a cry.

He was silent. Then he said, "I'm sorry."

They stood side by side and presently the young man took Lydia's hand and pulled her around facing him. "Look," he said gently, "let's admit it, you and I."

"Admit what?"

"We're two of a kind. We know that, don't we? I'm scouting for rich women. You're scouting for rich men. Tonight we've both lost out. Maybe we'll have better luck tomorrow. But tonight we're free. We have nothing to offer each other except each other—but we're both free tonight. So—why not?"

Lydia shuddered. "Oh!" she said. "No, no!"

She pulled away from him and turned in the other direction, away from the bar, toward the casino. She walked rapidly, clutching her purse. At the glass doors that led into the casino she stopped. The tables were beginning to fill up; she could hear the sound of the wheels, the mechanical clatter of the machines along the wall, the rattle of the *chemin de fer* cage, the chink of poker chips, and the tinkle of ice cubes in glasses. She hesitated. She could see the faces, faces of men intent upon the action of the tables, faces of the croupiers, faces of the girls, and suddenly, even from the distance at which she stood, every face seemed cruel. The faces did not seem clouded with greed or desperation but with evil and brutality. And in the whole brightly lighted room full of sounds and occasional bursts of laughter, there was not a single face that looked kind. She turned and leaned her back heavily against the glass door.

The young man was walking away from her toward the cocktail lounge. She watched him.

Then she called, "Don."

He stopped and turned.

"Wait!" she called. She arranged her face in her best smile. "Wait for Lydia!"

THE SNOWS OF YOUTH

✿✿✿✿ When Ellen Brier opened her eyes that morning the air was so clear and so pure that she had the sensation of having somehow awakened in the center of a crystal paperweight. Trapped in this prism with her were all the things from the night before: her yellow robe tossed over the chair, her sandals on the woven rug, her three suitcases packed and ready to go. The curtains hung absolutely still and in the window the green wing of an ipomoea vine cast a gray shadow of stems and marbly veins on the white sheets. There were no sounds. Then she began to hear the muffled morning noises of the hotel— the maids murmuring soft Cruzan words, soft bare footsteps padding across the stone terrace, the *rush-rush* sound of their brooms, and the gentle chink of china as the terrace tables were set for breakfast—the last breakfast before the hotel closed for the season. Yesterday, Ellen thought, I would not have felt this wonderful excitement about going home; I would have dreaded it. But today she felt almost absurdly happy. She stepped out of bed and went to the window.

Below, the little terrace was in a puddle of sunlight, gleaming whitely like a pale linen handkerchief thrown down. Around it, tubs and pots of geraniums and lobelia spilled pink and blue. A shower of purple-red hibiscus shot upward against the white clay wall of the kitchen house. She saw Mrs. Carmichael's tall, straight-backed chair, empty now, where Mrs. Carmichael sat every day, stiff and erect in her black lace-bosomed dress, her hands busy with her knitting, her white head nodding in rhythm with her needles, her tiny old-lady's feet in black hose and black buttoned shoes planted squarely in front of her. Nothing stirred in the light but the plantain leaves in the warm breeze. Ellen turned away from the window and walked back to the bed. She lay down again and pulled the sheet over her toes. She glanced at her travel clock; it was quarter past seven. In three more hours she would be on the plane. Six hours after that she would be home. And best of all, she thought, she had a goal. It was as though Mrs. Carmichael had handed her a goal with her small, wrinkled hand.

Ellen's friendship with Mrs. Carmichael began strangely, with the old lady's brandishing her black walking stick over Ellen's head.

"Young lady, do you realize where you are sitting?" Mrs. Carmichael had said. And then, commandingly, "Get up!"

Ellen had jumped to her feet. "I'm terribly sorry," she stammered.

Without a word Mrs. Carmichael had seated herself in the chair, carefully tucking her black skirts around her knees and placing her walking stick on the arm of the chair. Finally, when she was completely settled, she looked up at Ellen. "How do you do?" she said. "I am Mrs. Edward Carmichael."

"I'm—I'm Ellen Brier."

"You must be new here at the hotel," the old lady said. "This is my chair. I say *my* chair because it is actually my own chair.

It is not the hotel's property. I purchased this chair myself and had it shipped down here from New York. It was especially designed to support my back."

"Really, I'm awfully sorry."

"Don't mention it," Mrs. Carmichael said crisply. "You had no way of knowing. But now you know." She picked up her knitting bag and placed it on her lap. "From three to four every afternoon I walk. During that hour this chair is available for any guest of the hotel who wishes to sit in it. But I expect it relinquished by four sharp. I assume you found it comfortable."

"I did," Ellen said. "Very."

"It is probably the only one of its kind." Mrs. Carmichael began to knit rapidly—a signal, Ellen was to learn later, that the conversation was closed.

For the next few days Ellen avoided Mrs. Carmichael carefully. She told her mother about the incident, and Ellen and her mother enjoyed speculating about Mrs. Carmichael's presence at the hotel.

"I think she's a famous ax murderess," Ellen had said. "She's come to the Virgin Islands to escape the law."

"She comes from Newburyport, Massachusetts," Ellen's mother had said.

"How on earth did you find that out?"

"She has a Newburyport paper mailed to her. I've seen her pick it up."

"But why in the world would a little old lady like that come down here?" Ellen asked. "She doesn't go near the beach. She hates the sun—she pushes that chair into the shadiest spot she can find. I've heard her complaining about the food—"

"She's been here for a long time," Mrs. Brier said. "They told me that at the desk."

"Aha! Then you've been doing a little detective work your-self."

"Well," Ellen's mother said, "she doesn't seem like the kind of person one would expect to find . . ."

That afternoon Ellen had been walking back from the beach when she met Mrs. Carmichael on the path. She murmured, "Good afternoon," stepping to one side to let Mrs. Carmichael pass. To Ellen's surprise, Mrs. Carmichael stopped, looked up at her, and smiled brightly. "Well, my dear," she said, "are you enjoying yourself?"

"Very much," said Ellen.

Mrs. Carmichael leaned on her cane. "Is that your mother who is with you?"

"Yes."

"A most attractive woman. Where is your father?"

"My father isn't living," Ellen said.

"I see," said Mrs. Carmichael without pausing. "Why are you here?"

"I beg your pardon?"

"Why are you here? Why did you come to St. Croix? You're far too pretty to be stuck in this Godforsaken spot. There are no young men on this island."

"Well," Ellen faltered, "I—I came here for a rest."

"A rest? You don't look tired. You look as healthy as a horse. Where is your home?"

"In Connecticut."

"Ah, that's a familiar state. A very familiar state. I am from Newburyport, Massachusetts. Do you know Newburyport?"

"No, I've never been there," Ellen said.

"It's cold in winter. That's why I winter here. I have wintered here for thirty years. If you wish, you may finish my walk with me. I walk down there"—she pointed with her cane—"and then I turn and circle back by the lookout hill."

Ellen found herself falling into slow step beside Mrs. Carmichael. For most of the walk the old lady was silent. But she would stop occasionally to point out a particular landmark—a tree or a ruin or a stretch of sea view where a ship had gone down—and with these comments she would supply bits of island history. "There was once a fine harbor at Christiansted," she said. "But they have let it become clogged with mud. Laziness."

Gradually Ellen found herself enjoying the old lady—her quick, imperious gestures with her cane, her abrupt, almost rude questions, and her quick, unexpected smiles. They were almost back to the hotel when Mrs. Carmichael placed a hand on Ellen's arm. "You still haven't told me," she said.

"Told you what?"

"You haven't told me why you came here. I don't believe it was for a rest. You might as well tell me—I'll find out sooner or later. I make it a point to know everything about everybody who comes to the hotel."

Ellen laughed. "Very well," she said. "I came here to forget."

"Ah. That's more like it. To forget whom?"

"A young man. I was engaged."

"Yes. And what happened?"

"The engagement was broken."

"By whom? By you or by him?"

"It was—it was a mutual thing," Ellen said. "It wouldn't have worked out."

"Why not, may I ask?"

"We—we had different backgrounds."

"Poppycock. What difference does that make?"

Ellen was suddenly flustered. "He—he wanted to be a school-teacher."

"What's wrong with that?"

"For one thing, there's no money in it," Ellen said lamely.

"What? I'm surprised at you! What an absurd answer!"

"No," Ellen said, "I don't mean that. But—well, that's what my mother said, and it's just one reason—"

"Your mother. Did she break it off?"

"Really," Ellen said, "there's no point in our discussing it. There were many reasons, believe me."

"But your mother. Tell me what she wanted."

"You have to understand Mother," Ellen said. "She's a wonderful woman, really she is. But she's a businesswoman. I mean, she took over Daddy's business after he died. She really made it what it is today. She's always hoped I'd marry someone who would go into the business. Jimmy couldn't care less about it. All he wants is to be a schoolteacher. Even a college teacher would have sounded better to Mother—but Jimmy wants to be a grammar-school teacher! He doesn't care about making money. He and Mother quarreled badly—" She broke off. "Why am I telling you all this?" she asked.

"Because I don't beat around the bush," said Mrs. Carmichael. "Did you love him?"

Ellen was silent a moment. "Yes, I think so," she said finally. "Jimmy is a funny person. Not handsome, I suppose, but intelligent and kind. He's sort of an idealist . . ."

"I assume you're rich," Mrs. Carmichael said abruptly, her pale blue eyes looking up sharply at Ellen.

"Why, I—"

"Are you?" Mrs. Carmichael snapped. "Answer me."

"Well, yes, I suppose you might say—"

"Don't apologize," Mrs. Carmichael said. "I am rich too. Much richer than you, I'll wager. And of course he is poor."

"Yes."

"Rich is rich and poor is poor, and never the twain shall meet," she said. "Ah, *les neiges de jeunesse.*"

"Pardon me?"

"*Les neiges de jeunesse*—the snows of youth. An expression I use. How old are you—twenty-one, twenty-two?" Without waiting for Ellen to answer, she said, "Come along. It's nearly four o'clock." They started up the path to the hotel.

That evening Ellen's mother came to her room. "Would you zip me up please, dear?" she asked, turning the back of her pale-green sheath toward Ellen. "I can't find my nail polish. Did you borrow it?"

"No," Ellen said. She pulled up her mother's zipper.

"I strongly suspect these native maids," Mrs. Brier said. "My perfume has been disappearing at the rate of an inch a day. I'm sure the polish was on my dresser this morning before the maid did the room."

"Mother," Ellen said, "did you know Jimmy wrote me a letter yesterday?"

"No, dear, I didn't. What did he have to say?"

"It was just—nothing. Just a letter."

"Surely you're not going to answer it, Ellen."

"I don't know. . . ."

Mrs. Brier turned to her. "Ellen," she said, "you wouldn't do such a thing, would you? It's ended, isn't it? The whole problem is settled. Why keep reopening it?"

"I just don't know, Mother."

"Oh, Ellen, please, don't talk like this! There's nothing more to it, can't you see?"

"Mother, what's wrong with being a schoolteacher?"

"Well, in the first place—"

"I know," Ellen said sharply. "There's no money in it! But what else is wrong?"

Mrs. Brier turned away. "Oh, Ellen," she said, "I wanted so much more for you. So much more!"

"I know, Mother," Ellen said quickly. "I'm sorry."

"Just don't *think* about Jimmy any more. Come on, let's have a cocktail before dinner. I met some people named Kent this afternoon. Quite attractive, from Chicago. They mentioned bridge with us tonight. Would you like that?"

That night Ellen and her mother played bridge with Mr. and Mrs. Kent. Mr. Kent was large and boisterous; Mrs. Kent was small and complaining. The evening seemed long, and Ellen finally excused herself and went to her room. She made it a point to look at the letter again, not to read it, not even to think about Jimmy. But that night, quite late, she awakened and began to cry, and was unable to sleep again.

As the days went by, Ellen met Mrs. Carmichael often on her walks. She began to time her return from the beach in the afternoon to find Mrs. Carmichael on the path. Mrs. Carmichael's walking schedule proceeded as regularly as clockwork, and always when they met the old lady seemed genuinely pleased to see Ellen.

"You're one of the few promising people at this hotel," Mrs. Carmichael said once. "Have you looked at the rest of them?"

"Well, Mother sees a lot of the Kents, and I've met that Mrs. Arnold."

"They have no promise, any of them. The Kents—he's an excommunicated priest. Did you know that?"

"No."

"And Mrs. Arnold came down here to get a divorce, but she's taken her time about getting it. She wants the house and the car and the bank account, and Mr. Arnold doesn't seem to want to give them to her. No promise, any of them."

"Really, you do know the most amazing things about people!"

"I have nothing else to occupy me," Mrs. Carmichael said simply.

Periodically she would look inquisitively at Ellen and say, "Well, have you forgotten yet?" If Ellen replied, "Yes," as she sometimes did, Mrs. Carmichael would shake her head and say, "No, you haven't." And if Ellen said, "No," which was after all closer to the truth, Mrs. Carmichael would say, "Well, it takes time, I suppose."

Bit by bit, in fragments and pieces, Mrs. Carmichael told Ellen about herself. "My father was a Dane," she said. "A long time ago he owned this island—most of it. He came here as a poor boy from Denmark and exploited the natives. Why beat around the bush? That's what he did. He ended up owning the lighter fleet, a sugar plantation—the old mill up there was his. He owned the bank and most of the shops. He was ruthless."

"Then you were brought up here."

"Yes. I have lived through twenty hurricane seasons and I'll never live through another one. I went to Newburyport when I was twenty-one. Now I come here only during the good season and leave before it starts to blow. You wouldn't enjoy the island through a hurricane—it's dreadful. We had storm shutters two inches thick. Now that this is a tourist island, all the hotels close to let the hurricanes go through."

"Yes. That's when we go home."

"I'm eighty," Mrs. Carmichael said. "That seems old to you, doesn't it? My father lived to be ninety-three. The natives said he was too mean to die—neither the Almighty nor the devil wanted him. He always wore a white silk ascot with a black ivory cameo pinned in the center of it. He was very handsome and very vain."

"He must have been a remarkable man," Ellen said.

"You might say that," said Mrs. Carmichael.

"Was your husband—Mr. Carmichael—from here?" Ellen asked.

"Edward? No, no. He was from Newburyport. He was a sea captain. He sailed down here and we were married here."

"How romantic!" Ellen said.

"Yes. I suppose you'd call it a whirlwind courtship."

"And he took you back to Newburyport?"

"No, we lived here. He went to work for my father, with the lighter fleet. We were going to build a house."

"And what happened?"

"He died," said Mrs. Carmichael simply.

"Oh, I'm terribly sorry," Ellen said gently.

"It was very long ago," Mrs. Carmichael said. "Come on, it's nearly four o'clock." They went toward the hotel in silence. Then, just at the last turn in the path, Mrs. Carmichael stopped. "Why do you always meet me at the end of my walk?" she asked.

"Because it's on my way back from the beach."

Mrs. Carmichael snorted. "The beach! The sea holds too

many bodies. Someday I'll take you on the beginning of my walk. I start there"—she raised her cane and pointed—"and I go to the top of the hill, then down."

"I'd love to go with you," Ellen said.

"Well, one day I may ask you," Mrs. Carmichael said crisply. As they came within view of the hotel terrace, she whispered, "Look. There's that Kent man in my chair. I shall tell him to stay out of it."

That night as they sat having dinner Mrs. Brier turned to Ellen and said, "Darling, why *do* you spend so much time with that peculiar old woman?"

"Why, I think she's rather sweet, Mother."

"Honestly, you're always walking around with her. Aren't you having fun?"

"Of course I am."

"Well, really, dear, it does look awfully funny. You never talk to anyone except her. I'm afraid people will think you're as barmy as she is!"

"She's not barmy!"

"Well, it certainly is grotesque. A young girl spending all her time with a decrepit old lady in a long black dress and black stockings. John Kent remarked to me just this afternoon—"

"Mr. Kent! I could tell you a few things about him!"

Mrs. Brier leaned forward eagerly. "What?" she asked. "What have you learned? He's most attractive, don't you think?"

"Never mind, Mother," Ellen said. "It was nothing at all."

It was several days before Mrs. Carmichael mentioned her husband or her past again. Then one afternoon, meeting Ellen in the usual place at the end of her walk, she said, her eyes twinkling, "Well, how are you today? Have you forgotten? Is it yes or no today?"

"It's no today, I'm afraid," Ellen said.

"Any more letters from him?"

"Yes, one."

"Have you answered it?"

"No."

"You're a namby-pamby!"

Ellen laughed. "Are you trying to play Cupid?" she asked.

"Don't be silly. I wouldn't dream of doing such a thing. Everyone must work out his own salvation." Then she switched the subject abruptly. "That was Edward's great fault," she said.

"What was?"

"He let others make his decisions for him."

"Oh?"

"Yes. He had a certain amount of courage but no grit, if you see the difference. When he died he died courageously. But it was without grit."

"I don't believe you told me how he died," Ellen said.

"Of course I didn't, I'm quite aware of that. Do you think I'd tell you everything about myself in one breath? You'd soon find me very uninteresting if I didn't hold out a little something. You wouldn't join me on my walks."

"That's not true," Ellen said. "I walk with you because I like you."

"Say what you may," Mrs. Carmichael said. "Well, Edward. Edward died in a duel."

"A duel!"

"Yes." She smiled slyly. "I thought you'd like that! Well, it's quite true. Poor man, he was shot in a duel."

"How terrible!"

"It was long ago," said Mrs. Carmichael. "And it was a foolish way to die. No grit. They both died. Edward was only twenty-nine, one of the youngest captains to sail out of New-buryport."

"Who was the other man?"

"The Frenchman. A Frenchman who came here to the is-land."

"What was the reason for it?" Ellen asked.

"Well," Mrs. Carmichael said, "when I was a girl I was con-sidered a beauty. Why beat around the bush? I was. Edward and I had been married only a little while, and the Frenchman came. I caught his eye . . ."

"Oh, I see," said Ellen softly.

"The Frenchman. He was very headstrong—the French are a headstrong race. But it was not his idea to duel. Whose fault was it? I don't know. Some might say it was my fault—but I have my own reasons for knowing that it wasn't."

"What did your father say?"

"Father? Mercy me, he was all for it! He gave them the pis-tols. He was right in the middle of it. He was in his glory!"

"And what did you do? Couldn't you stop them?"

"No. They made me stay out of it. I waited on the veranda. It was early in the morning. I waited. I heard the shots. Then Father came riding back on his horse to give me the news. Both of them. Each man killed with the other's first shot."

"How dreadful for you!"

"Yes, I won't deny it was. Dreadful. But, then, the Almighty gives us years to forget how dreadful things are. Gracious, it was sixty years ago."

Ellen put her arm around the old lady's shoulders. "My poor dear," she said. "That's why you come back, then. The snows of youth . . ."

Mrs. Carmichael suddenly looked up at the sky. "Do you

notice any difference?" she asked. "No? I do. In two weeks, maybe three, the hurricanes will be here. I can smell it. I can see it by the way the sky looks. The natives can tell it too. Have you noticed? They're bringing out the storm shutters for the hotel. It closes in another week, and I'll go back to Newburyport. Where will you go?"

"Home," said Ellen sadly. "I don't want to go."

"Afraid to see him again?"

"Yes."

"Take what comes," Mrs. Carmichael said. And then she added cryptically, "Take what comes—up to a certain point. Come along."

And now, lying in her bed in that crystalline morning, thinking about it, Ellen tried to picture the long-ago scene. The young and beautiful Mrs. Carmichael on the veranda, in white (surely it must have been white), standing erect to hear the dreadful news as her father, the Danish planter, rode up, tall and dashing, on his horse. The scene was like watching an old-fashioned pantomime. From the open window she tried to hear the echo of pistol shots—two shots fired so close together they were almost one, but not quite.

Yesterday afternoon, right after lunch, there had been a knock on her door as Ellen was dressing for the beach. She threw a robe over her bathing suit and went to the door. Mrs. Carmichael was standing there. She had never come to Ellen's room before.

"Well, my dear," the old lady had said, "do you realize what day it is? This is our last full day here. Hurry up."

"Where are we going?"

"I promised I'd take you on the beginning of my walk. Come along."

"All right," Ellen said. She slipped on a pair of sandals, and still wearing her yellow terry beach robe, followed Mrs. Carmichael along the narrow balcony that skirted the second floor of the hotel and down the broad stone steps that led to the terrace.

They started along a little path that led through a grove of banana trees and up the hill toward the sugar mill. "My father's mill," Mrs. Carmichael said, pointing with her cane. "The lizards own it now." They went a little farther. "The house was here," she said. "It burned in a great fire a long time ago."

Then they went down the other side of the hill, through another banana grove, through a broad field where lazy donkeys grubbed in the dried brown grass. "All sugar cane once," Mrs. Carmichael said. Then they came to a tall tree and Mrs. Carmichael stopped there.

"It was here," she said. "It was under this very tree they fought." She prodded the earth with the top of her black cane. "It was on this very patch of ground." She looked upward. "Under this very sun, I suppose." Her eyes gleamed brightly, but there were no tears.

"Why do you come here?" Ellen whispered. "Why do you torture yourself like this?"

"You!" Mrs. Carmichael snapped. "You said you came here to forget. I come here to remember!"

"But it was so long ago."

"It doesn't make any difference," she said. "I come here because I hope someday to die here, where he died."

"But you mustn't," Ellen said. "You mustn't do this to yourself."

Mrs. Carmichael's voice was far away. "It was right here," she said. "A duel. What a foolish way to die. I took Edward's body back to Newburyport. It was what he had wanted. It was winter, and everything was frozen. My heart was frozen too."

"And you stayed in Newburyport to be near him."

"No. Because I had nowhere else to go. I hated every memory of Newburyport, but I couldn't come back here while my father still lived. And he lived for a long time. I had to wait nearly thirty years for him to die—until, at last—"

"But I don't understand," Ellen said.

"It was thirty years before I could come back to where he died. His grave is here somewhere. Father never marked it."

"But who—"

"The Frenchman. I loved the Frenchman. Father made me marry Edward—a business arrangement. He was getting too old to command the lighter fleet himself, he said—though he went on commanding it for thirty years, after Edward. He wanted Edward. They were very much alike, Father and Edward. But Edward hated the tropics, didn't want to stay. But when Father gave me to Edward, he agreed to stay."

"I see," said Ellen.

"A duel! Father's idea. Only the Frenchman was supposed to die. But they both died, and—ah, well, that was all right too, I suppose, with Father. I used to see him whip the blacks with the flat side of a machete. Look," Mrs. Carmichael said, turning suddenly to Ellen, "life is a sort of duel, it seems to me. Not a killing duel, but it is combat. You have to fight. A woman has to fight sometimes for what she wants. I never fought Father until it was too late. But you can fight if you have an ounce of grit. I mean marry that schoolteacher. Your mother is a fool. She's in love with that Kent man. Don't act so shocked. I've watched her. She'd marry him if he'd divorce his wife. But he won't. Go your own way. Marry the schoolteacher.

Come on, let's get back. I don't feel like finishing my walk today."

That night Mrs. Brier had come into Ellen's room. "Aren't you dressed, dear?" she asked. "Tonight's the farewell cocktail party. Everyone's gathering downstairs on the terrace."

"I don't think I'll go, Mother," Ellen said.

"Why not, for heaven's sake? Darling, you've been a stick-in-the-mud this whole trip. Won't you at least put in an appearance tonight?"

Ellen crossed the room to the window and looked out. Below, the cocktail party—the last cocktail party of the last night of the season—was under way. Mr. Kent, in Mrs. Carmichael's chair, was doing an imitation of Mrs. Carmichael, pretending to be pounding the stones with a cane. There was a roar of laughter.

"Hurry *up,* dear," Mrs. Brier said.

"I have things to do tonight," Ellen said.

"Ellen, what's come over you?" Mrs. Brier asked. "Will you please snap out of it and slip on a dress and come downstairs?"

"I'm going to write Jimmy a letter, for one thing," she said.

"Ellen!"

"I'm going to write Jimmy a letter."

"Please stop that sort of talk."

Ellen turned and faced her mother. "I am," she said. "And I'm going to tell him just what you're afraid I'm going to tell him."

Mrs. Brier, in her blue silk print, stood there folding and unfolding her hands. Finally she turned on her heel and walked out of the room. "I wash my hands of you!" she said.

For a while Ellen had watched the party on the terrace. Mrs. Arnold arrived, wearing a bright native-print skirt. There was her mother with the Kents. It was growing noisy; voices were pitched higher, full of expectancy for what the evening held. Gathered there, by their very intimacy they seemed to draw a curtain around themselves that excluded everything beyond them. There is only us, they seemed to be saying. There is nothing but this terrace, this evening, these cocktails, this talk.

Standing at her window, Ellen noticed that everyone on the terrace faced inward, toward one another, their backs turned against everything that lay outside.

The sun was going down. No one watched it as it started its swift, spectacular slide into the sea. They were like a herd of pigeons in a park, Ellen thought, all pecking at the scattered kernels of conversation. This conceit pleased her, somehow. It would please Jimmy too. It was strange to think that in the morning they would all have flown away.

WATER WON'T QUENCH FIRE

✿✿✿✿ Dolly looked out the living-room window and said, Now wasn't that the limit? It was going to rain. Wasn't that just like up-North weather? But when no one answered her she turned around and saw that Barbara had stepped into the kitchen and was out of earshot. With great care Dolly took a cigarette out of the silver box on the coffee table, lit it, and inhaled deeply. Then she picked up the box and examined the hallmark on the bottom. "Sterling!" she murmured appreciatively.

"Of course," said Barbara, coming in again with two bottles of beer and glasses. "Jeff picked it out. Want a beer?"

"Oh, you know I don't drink, dear!" said Dolly.

Barbara set the bottles down. "You don't? Since when?"

"Oh, since a long, long time."

"Not even a beer? To celebrate your arrival?"

Dolly lifted her left wrist and glanced at the tiny egg-shaped watch that dangled among the bracelets. "W-e-e-ll," she said, extending the vowel and punctuating it with a sharp stream of smoke, "it *is* three o'clock." She laughed nervously. "It's *almost* the cocktail hour. I'll have one, just one."

Barbara emptied the beer into the glasses and handed one to Dolly. Dolly took her glass, and skirted the coffee table to the sofa. Barbara crossed the room to a small, pink velvet chair; with one hand, she fished inside the pocket of her pale-gray shantung shirt. "Got a cigarette?" she asked.

"Why, Barb, there are thousands of them here in this box." She reached for the box, opened it, and tossed a cigarette to her sister. "*Catch!*" she yelled, and screamed hysterically as Barbara grabbed for it and missed.

Barbara reached down and picked up the cigarette from the floor.

"Hey," she said, "take it easy."

Dolly sat back in her chair, her shoulders shaking. "Sorry, Barb," she said.

"You seem kind of nervous," Barbara said, looking at her.

"Do I? Maybe I am. Seeing you again and all."

Barbara picked up one of the table lighters and lit her cigarette. "Stale," she said. "Jeff likes to keep cigarettes around in boxes. He thinks it's *classy,* or something. He doesn't mind if they get stale. He doesn't smoke."

For a moment or two the two sisters sat smoking, studying each other, saying nothing. Dolly fidgeted with a silver charm bracelet. She was the older girl, but the soft afternoon light in the living room flattered her and softened her features, so that she might easily have been mistaken for the younger. Her hair, which was not its own color, was drawn back from her face more severely than Barbara's, which fell in natural blonde waves. And her skin, clouded now under makeup, was pale. Her eyes were deepened with mascara. Barbara, who was just twenty-five, had a fuller face and figure. Her mouth was possibly a bit too wide, but she did her best to correct this feature by holding her lips in a manner that might have suggested a pout—a pout on a pretty face. Still, if someone had walked into that room at that moment he would have seen at first glance two emphatic young women. But this impression would not have been final. Dolly's pallor would have emerged later; Barbara's wide, friendly smile would have erased the sulky look and replaced it with a look of unaffected naturalness.

"Well," Barbara said, smiling now, "how've you been? You look fine, just fine."

"Me?" Dolly asked. "Oh, I'm just blooming. The Florida sunshine was just what the doctor ordered." She picked up her glass and sipped from it. With the toe of her black pump she began a little rhythmic tapping on the rug. She crooked a silver-tipped finger and scratched the monogram that had been traced on the side of the glass. "Expensive," she said.

Barbara laughed dryly. "Sure, everything here's expensive. Look at my shoes." She extended one foot. "They were *very* expensive. Jeff likes things that way. Did you expect to find me living in squalor?"

"Oh, no!" Dolly exclaimed. "Of course not. But it's been such a long time. Three years, actually, since I've seen you. And when I last saw you Jeff was—you know—just getting started. Just struggling along." She paused a moment. "I suppose he must be making all sorts of money now."

"He does all right," Barbara said. "We get along."

"Your home is—well, it's *beautiful,* Barb. Really, from the way you described it in your letter, I thought—"

"You should see some of the houses around here," Barbara said. "This place is nothing. I'll give you our twenty-five-cent tour of New Hope tomorrow. They say here that the mechanics live on Ferry Street and the fairies live on Mechanic Street. Tomorrow, we'll go out and laugh at the natives."

"Well, I'd certainly like that," Dolly said absently.

"You'd turn green."

"Yes."

"How was your trip?"

"My trip? Up here? Dreadful. All the way up in the plane I sat beside some terrible little I-don't-know-*what* with a bag of sandwiches!" She laughed. "And I think he must have taken a shine to me, Barb, because he kept offering—oh, well! Never mind the dreary details. Suffice it to say I'm here. And tired!"

"It's wonderful to see you again, Dolly."

"Yes. Now, why did you ask me to come?"

"Hmm?"

"Why did you want me to come? I mean, I'm delighted to see you, Barb. And it was sweet of you to send me the ticket. But I mean, why so sudden—after three years? You sounded so urgent in your letter—"

Barbara stood up and flipped her cigarette into the fireplace. Then she went to the sofa and plunked herself down beside Dolly. "I need your advice," she said finally.

"You need *my* advice? About what?"

"I'm thinking about divorcing Jeff."

Dolly gulped her beer. "*What?*" she asked.

"Yes. It's—well, it's a long story. It just doesn't seem to be working out, that's all. And you—you've been through the mill, Dolly. You've been divorced. I thought maybe you could give me some pointers."

"Pointers?"

"Yes. How. Where. How much. Et cetera."

"Are you serious, Barb?"

"Sure I'm serious."

"Barb!"

"What?"

"I don't know what's come over you. You sound so—so callous. You sound as hard as nails."

Barbara laughed. "Maybe I'm in with a bad crowd."

"Well! I don't know, I just don't. I'm shocked, actually."

"You never really expected it would work out, did you? Me, married to Mr. Suburbia, U.S.A.? A knight in shining black *attaché* case? Do you know why we live way the hell out here? Because he thinks that the farther away from the city you live the richer you look. So he spends nearly four hours a day on the goddam train."

"Don't talk that way," Dolly said. "Please." She paused. "I mean—don't you love him?"

Barbara picked up her glass and held it in front of her face, staring through the amber liquid. "Love him? Oh, I love him, I suppose." She looked sharply at her sister. "You loved Danny, didn't you?"

"Is there another woman, as we say?"

"Ha!" Barbara said. "I doubt it. He's too hooked on status to take on another woman. It wouldn't *look* right, you see."

"Oh dear."

"And besides he's too busy. He's very *busy* being busy because that's the way you get ahead, says he—by being busy. Work all day—come home at night and work some more." She turned and looked at Dolly. "Do you realize that it's been weeks since he and I have had an intelligent conversation? About anything? He's so wrapped up in his everlasting business deals that he doesn't have time for anything else."

"But you said he takes an interest in this house."

"This house! Oh, yes, that's another story. Do you know why he takes an interest in this house—why he likes things like silver cigarette boxes? Like all this stuff?" She gestured around her. "It's because he thinks they're an asset to the damn business. He thinks this is the way we *ought* to be living."

"Oh."

"And I've got a feeling that's what he thinks *I* am—another damned cigarette box. That's why he takes such an interest in how I dress. Oh, he's generous! But it can't be *me* he's thinking about."

"But you do love him."

"Well, I just said. You loved Danny, didn't you?"

Dolly took a swallow of her drink. "Oh, yes," she said softly.

"So you see?" Barbara stood up, her glass in her hand.

"Where are you going?"

"We're out of beer. I'm going to fix us something serious to drink."

"Barbara, do you think you should? I mean it's only three o'clock, and—"

"Quiet. I'm getting us a drink." She walked out of the room and banged open the kitchen door in the distance.

"Oh dear," said Dolly to herself, looking again out the window. "It *is* raining." She rose and stood uncertain for a moment, then stepped to the chair where she had left her bag. She removed her compact and, with a small soft brush, dabbed at her cheeks. "A fright, a fright," she whispered to her image in the tiny mirror.

When Barbara came back Dolly was sitting on the sofa, stroking a cushion with one hand. "I love your slip covers, Barb," she said. "Where did you get them made?"

"I don't know," said Barbara. "Somewhere."

"They're lovely."

"Yeah. Here's your drink," Barbara said, handing her a glass.

Dolly looked up innocently. "Oh, did you fix *me* one? I couldn't touch it. Really, honey, I never take anything stronger than beer."

"Shut up and take it."

Dolly hesitated, then took the glass and tasted the liquor. "Well," she said, "it *is* refreshing. What is it? Scotch?"

"Bourbon."

"Oh. Well, you can see I'm no connoisseur. Now if I say or do anything silly—"

"I'll forgive you," Barbara said. "You can do no wrong. Blood is thicker than water."

"Or bourbon?" Dolly asked, and giggled. She took another sip.

"I suppose it is funny," Barbara said.

"What is?"

"Me. Getting a divorce. I suppose it doesn't strike you as being very serious."

"Now, Barb," Dolly said, "don't get scoldy. You said you wanted my advice. Now, please, just let me think about it for a minute or two. I want to have time to mull it over a bit." She began the little tapping again with her foot.

"Mull away," Barbara said. She went to the sofa, sat down, and kicked off her low-heeled sandals. "And stop that," she said.

"What?"

"That tapping thing you're doing. It drives me crazy."

"Sorry."

Some time later Dolly's eyes were shining, and she was saying, "Well, as I just said, I got a divorce. But I was only twenty-two, twenty-three then. I'm thirty-seven now. If I were getting a divorce now, I might do it differently."

"Thirty-*seven*? How differently?"

"Well—differently. Like, maybe not get a divorce at all."

"You mean you wish you hadn't?"

"Oh, no. No, I'm glad, I suppose. At the time, it seemed like the right thing to do. Danny was—oh, you know how Danny was."

"A lush."

"Oh, yes, that—but—"

"You mean you're sorry now."

"Oh, I don't know about sorry—" She broke off suddenly. "That plant," she said, pointing. "It's huge—what is it?"

"Huh? Oh, I don't know. Some damn thing."

"It's beautiful. Does it blossom?"

"Sure, I guess it blossoms. If I remember to water it. Guess who brought it home with him one afternoon. And set it right *there*. For me to take care of. Guess."

"But it's pretty!"

"Don't change the subject. You're a damn subject-changer, you know that?"

"Oh, but I keep thinking—you have this pretty house, all these expensive things. They must count for something, Barb. If I had all this—"

Barbara spoke earnestly. "Look," she said, "do you remember when you came home that time in Cleveland, after being with

Danny? Do you remember what you told Mother? Oh, I know I was still pretty young, but I remember. You said, 'Mother, I'm bored, bored with being married. I want to be a free agent.' "

"Bored! But I was only twenty-*two*!"

"Well, that's exactly what I want to be—a free agent. I want—it may sound silly—but I want to have fun. Perhaps a little career. Like you've had. Look at you these past few years. You've been to Europe, South America, California—now Florida—"

"Oh, yes, yes," Dolly interrupted. "Yes, of course it's fun. And gay. No, don't think I'm bored any more. And I've had my little flings. But it's kind of—tenuous? Is that the right word? What I mean is it's uncertain. And don't think that because I live in Florida I have a mansion or something on Collins Avenue. I've been living in a greasy little walk-up apartment where all the exhaust fumes from the street come right up through my window—and—" She stopped abruptly. "Oh, I've had *fun*," she went on. "I go to parties all the time, nearly every night. Remember how popular I was in Cleveland? Well, I'm still popular. I have lots of friends. Lots of men. When you get your divorce, Barb, you'll find there are lots of men. They'll *swarm* around. They'll take you out, buy you drinks. But do they want to marry you? No. Ha-ha." She took a swallow of her drink. "Now I've got to go somewhere else."

"What are you talking about?"

"I didn't tell you this, Barb. I wasn't going to mention it right away. But I'm not going back to Florida."

"Really? Why not?"

"Well," Dolly said, "it's funny the way things work out. You see, just before I got your letter, asking me to come up—

just before that, I was going to write you. I was going to ask
you if I *could* come."

"Why?"

"Difficulties. No, not financial difficulties—I've got about
a thousand dollars saved. But—well, I had to quit my job."

"But I thought—"

"My employer—remember the man I told you about before?
Well, your sister was called a homewrecker!" Dolly laughed.
"Imagine! A homewrecker! Oh, and a few more slightly less
printable things. At least that's what his wife called me. Oh,
sure, he and I went out on dates. We went to parties and things.
He—he misled me a little. I thought he was separated, or something. But he wasn't."

"Oh."

"So—if you want the whole, ugly truth, I'm slightly *persona
non grata* in the state of Florida. I mean there's actually going
to be some sort of legal action, I guess. Corespondent—that's
what I'm being called. And then there's the stupid money
thing—I don't even understand it."

"What money thing?"

"Oh, some *things*—just bits of paper. Stocks or something
that he gave me, and now she's claiming that they weren't his
to give, that they were hers—I don't even pretend to know what
it's all about. So, anyway, when I got your letter—and your
plane ticket and all—I thought, What a stroke of luck! You
must have been psychic! Isn't that a riot—the coincidence?"
With a little nervous gesture, Dolly pushed her hair back from
her temple with one hand.

There was a silence, and Dolly looked at her sister. Barbara
sat, gently sloshing the ice cubes to and fro in her empty glass.

"So, I thought I'd swiftly and silently steal away before little Mrs. Simpson really decided to bare her fangs," Dolly said. "Honestly, Barb, you wouldn't believe the things she's been saying about me—and the evil letters his children have written to me, and even his grandson in Dallas—"

"*Grandson!*"

"Ed is a—a somewhat older man."

"Good lord."

"You're shocked, aren't you, Barb?"

"No."

"I can tell you are! But it's not as though you were harboring an actual criminal. I have a friend who's a lawyer in Miami, and he said that an alienation of affections, or whatever it is, is awfully hard to prove. I mean it's not as though there were *photographs*. And as for that stock, I accepted that in good faith—"

"Does he know you're here—this lawyer friend?"

Dolly laughed. "Not yet! I, as we say, skipped town. You *are* shocked."

"I'm not shocked. You're one of the family."

Dolly laughed again. "Yes," she said, "I guess we're two of a kind, Barb." She held up her glass. "Say, I think I'll have another of these if you don't mind."

Barbara looked at her for a moment. Then she said, "You bet," and stood up, a little unsteadily, and tried to push her feet into her shoes again. Then, unsuccessful at this, she walked barefoot into the kitchen.

"Lots of ice!" Dolly yelled after her, and when Barbara came back with the bottle in her hand, Dolly curled her feet up under her on the couch, and held her glass out playfully. Her mood had changed. "Don't let's be gloomy!" she cried. "Let's not sulk. Let's let bygones be bygones. After all, this isn't so bad, is it? Haven't we both been naughty little girls now and then? I remember once, Barb, when you were about fourteen—"

"Please be quiet," Barbara said sharply. "I'm trying to think."

"Oh, you'll love being divorced," Dolly said. "Go to Mexico where I got mine, and—"

"Please, *please!*"

"Barb?" Dolly said. "What's the matter? Are you shocked about me? Are you going to scold me—just because there's a little legal action—"

"Maybe Jeff could help you out."

"I don't need a lawyer *now*. I ran away! They can't do a thing to me here."

"I hope not."

"Besides, you're divorcing Jeff. Don't forget that."

"Yes."

"Oh, don't worry about little Dolly. She can take care of herself." Suddenly, she stood up.

"I—I don't know. I feel feverish. I—I may have caught cold on the plane. And these drinks—they seem to be affecting me. I'm not used to—" For an instant she tottered. "I think I'll take this upstairs with me and lie down. I'm tired." She put one foot quickly forward and caught her balance. "Do you mind, Barb? You can bring my things up later—"

Barbara stood up. "Of course I don't mind," she said. "I'll show you where your room is."

"Yes—I think I'd better."

Together they went out into the hall. Dolly started up the stairs first, her drink shaking and sloshing a little in her hand. "Isn't it funny?" she said. "The way things work out?" In a far-off voice she said, "Yes, this lovely house. This extensive

—I mean this *expensive*—everything—" She climbed the steps slowly, one by one, and at about the fifth step she started to fall, clutched at the banister for support, and then fell, haphazardly, awkwardly, face forward. The glass flew out of her hand onto the carpet and bounced, spilling crazily, down the steps. "Oh, oh, oh," she said.

"Here," Barbara said, reaching for her arm. "Here, love. Are you all right?" She pulled Dolly to her feet and, with her arm around her, continued up the stairs. At the top of the stairs, Dolly stopped, hesitated, and caught her breath. "If I can just lie down," she said.

"This way."

Barbara led her sister down the hall and opened the door to the guest bedroom. The wallpaper there was new, patterned with huge floating butterflies, and the Venetian blinds were down, tilted to keep out the sun. "Here we are," Barbara said. "Lie down and get some rest."

"Your carpet? Did I ruin your beautiful carpet?"

"Never mind about that." She led Dolly to the edge of the first twin bed and eased her onto it. Then she went to one of the windows, raised the blind, and turned and went over to the bed and sat on a corner of it. Dolly sat silently beside her, clutching her purse. "I shouldn't have given you those drinks," Barbara said.

"Beer and whiskey, mighty risky. Isn't that what we used to say?"

"Something like that."

All at once Dolly turned and gripped her sister by the shoulders, pressing her head hard into the curve of Barbara's throat. "Oh, Barb!" she cried. "Something's happened. Something's gone. I'm all changed. Don't believe me! Don't believe anything I say! You think I don't drink? I'm a liar. I drink. All the time. Look—" She fumbled with the clasp on her purse. "See?" she said, pulling out a flask. "My vodka. Want some? I've got more." She unscrewed the cap, and lifted the bottle to her lips. "Here's to us," she said, and drank.

"Oh, my dear." Barbara took the flask gently away from her, replaced the cap, and laid the flask on the bed between them.

"Look!" Dolly said. She was sobbing now. "Look at me. Look at what's happened to me. Maybe I was right to divorce Danny. But being married was something *certain*—the only certain thing I had. But then, afterward—oh, I just hope you're sure, awfully sure. I was only twenty-two, twenty-three! And ever since—things keep sliding, sliding away from me. Do you know what I'm like? Do you? I'm like the old woman. The old woman."

"Love?"

"The old woman who bought a pig. Remember the story Mother used to tell us? About the old woman who bought a pig? And the pig wouldn't go? Remember?"

"What? What?"

"Remember? The old woman told a dog to bite the pig—to make it go? And the dog wouldn't, and then she told a stick to beat the dog? And she kept going, going backward, to the next thing, and the next thing, farther and farther from what she wanted. Finally she called to the butcher—'Butcher, butcher, kill ox . . . ox won't drink water . . . water won't quench fire . . . fire won't burn stick . . . stick won't beat dog . . . dog won't bite pig. . . .' That's me. That's *me!* I can't find anyone to punish!" She fell forward across the pillows.

Barbara stood up. "Lie here," she said. "Just lie here. I know. I know."

"I keep going from one thing to another, and I'm getting farther and farther away from anything that makes any sense. Just slide—in a circle, you come back to where you started. I can't—"

"Hush, hush." Barbara stood up and rested her hand for a moment on Dolly's shoulder.

Then, softly, on tiptoe, she left the room, closed the door quietly behind her, and went down the stairs.

For a moment Dolly lay, her face buried in the satin bedspread, sobbing without sound. Then she sat up and looked around her. "No good, no good," she said. The flask lay on the bed beside her, where Barbara had placed it, and she picked it up. "Water won't quench fire," she said, and laughed. She unscrewed the cap again and quickly drank what remained, all at once. Then, with the empty flask still in her hand, she lay flat across the bed, on her back, and closed her eyes.

Downstairs Barbara wandered aimlessly through the rooms, doing little things, picking things up and setting them down again. In the living room she picked up the bottle and glasses and carried them into the kitchen and set the glasses in the sink. When she passed the stairs again she noticed the dark stain of whiskey on the carpet, and Dolly's glass on the floor. She returned to the kitchen, dampened a cloth, and went back to the foot of the stairs. For several minutes she worked on the stain, scrubbing it gently, fluffing up the damp nap of the carpet with her fingers. In the corner of the stairs, several ice cubes were dissolving into puddles; she picked these up, and then, after holding them a moment, cold and dripping, in her hand, she went into the living room and placed them carefully in the pot that held the plant. Then she made another trip to the kitchen and filled a pan with water, and went back to the plant again. She poured the water slowly, a little at a time, until the soil was soaked. Then she set the pan down. The house was silent, and the color had begun to drain from the day.

She wanted a cigarette; she went to the coffee table and picked up the polished box and held it for a moment in her hand, studying it. Then she lifted it quickly and pressed it to her cheek. The surface was smooth and cold; tears ran down. "Sterling," she whispered. She set the box down again, unopened.

She tried to remember where she had last used the portable downstairs telephone; then she remembered and went into the study. She dialed a number, and when a man answered immediately—after the first ring—she forgot for a moment what it was that she was going to say to him, if she had ever known, and suddenly her voice was choked and she could only make indistinguishable sounds into the mouthpiece. At last she said, "Jeff, I just called you up to hear your voice . . ."

STORM

✿✿✿✿ We are quite a cast of characters here, Linda thought dryly, quite a cast. She looked around at the group on the veranda: at Madame Foss, who owned the ramshackle old hotel which was called, almost too inappropriately, the Club Caprice, and who sat heavily in her wicker rocker, fanning her flushed and mottled face with a palm-leaf fan, her orange hair put up in rusty metal curlers; at Madras, who certainly must be part native—at least a mulatto, Linda thought—who called himself Madame Foss's husband (and perhaps he was), who wore old-fashioned steel-rimmed spectacles and drank Pointe-à-Pitre rum weakened with Coca-Cola, which he mixed himself, and carried about in miniature bottles that clinked in his trouser pockets; at Heaven Hill, the native maid, who was doing now a queer little shuffling dance step with an ancient dustcloth twisted between the toes of one bare foot. To these, she added herself: an American woman far from home whose husband was upstairs in their room where he had been for nearly a month with a fever that sometimes climbed as high as 104.

Heaven Hill moved across the rug, the dustcloth clenched between toes as prehensile as a monkey's, and dusted the nap and the bare thready places with the soles of her feet, singing "Umpah-umpah" under her breath.

"Does she have to do that?" Linda asked.

"Don't criticize," said Madame Foss, fanning herself and rocking backward in her chair. Her pink hat, which she had hung on the back of the chair when she returned from lobstering, fell to the floor with a little flop and lay there unheeded. "Dripping wet!" Madame Foss said in her voice that had a curious Cockney lilt to it. "Dripping wet. Press-piration it is. My first husband, the captain, used to say, 'Molly, you just *sweat.*' But I call it press-piration. Nobody knows how I suffer from it. Or cares." She began twisting the rings on her fingers —huge, improbable creations of paste and colored glass that Madame Foss stoutly insisted were diamonds, rubies, sapphires and emeralds, gifts of the late captain—and Linda looked out at the shifting sea that lapped soundlessly against the sea wall. The air was breathlessly still. She'd be cooler if she didn't wear all that junk jewelry, Linda thought, but she said nothing.

The island had been having monsoon weather all summer, but without wind. All through July it never rained, and not a breeze blew. It was like no West Indian summer in anyone's memory, and everyone had blamed it on the atomic bombs. "It's those bombs," they said, "it must be." Whatever it was, the mercury stayed in the hundreds week after week, the temperature outdoors matching, almost degree for degree, the heat in poor Harry's head. The barometer rose till it spilled green water over the spout, and the days fell away like sheets of paper. Even the young colored girls who sold rosettes of hibiscus and Judas flowers and orange pomanders and bunches of cha-cha leaves with the beans sticking out of them like long witch fingers during the tourist season—and who, for a long time after the season was over, had continued to try to sell their wares to Linda whenever she appeared on the street—even they had finally retreated from the heat into their thatched houses. The little donkey drivers from Basse-Terre came up the dusty path to the hotel with exceptional slowness, their legs splayed wide apart and dangling, singing mournfully about the heat. And everyone at the Club Caprice sat on the veranda try-ing not to move, day after day, waiting for the sun to go down a little, sometimes playing a little bridge or putting old calypso records on the wind-up victrola.

The natives insisted, too, that there was something wrong with the tides of Guadeloupe. With the ocean so still, huge sandbars had clogged the Rivière Salée, which divided the two main islands, and boat traffic between Basse-Terre and Grande Terre had ceased altogether. Harry's little French doctor made the trip on foot, across the mud. It was so hot that the date palms turned black at the tops, and the bougainvillea blossoms shriveled in the sun. I should go up and look in on him, Linda thought. But just the thought of stirring from the hammock exhausted her. She put her head in her hands.

"Cheer up! Cheer up!" said Madame Foss. "He's Libra, you know. I've read his stars. He'll be well within a three—three days, three weeks."

"Three months, three years," Linda said. *"Please.* Please let's not talk about that nonsense any more."

"It's *not* nonsense! If you'd let me read you, I could help you, baby. But you won't. You're as stubborn as the captain was."

Linda looked up at her. For what seemed like the hundredth time that day she said, "It's a simple question of money, Ma-dame Foss. That's all there is to it."

"Money isn't everything, baby," Madame Foss said.

Oh, damn her! Linda thought. She was impossible. You couldn't argue with her. Money isn't everything. If at first you don't succeed, try, try again. Live and learn. These were the maxims with which Madame Foss settled everything. "I need at least two hundred dollars," she said in a flat voice.

"Well, out of that you owe me a hundred and twenty rent," Madame Foss said. "That won't leave you much."

"How much did you get for selling his typewriter?" she asked. "Or don't I have a right to know?"

"We'll configurate that in when we settle the final bill," Madame Foss said. "That won't leave you much."

"I suppose I could treat that as an act of outright thievery, couldn't I?" Linda said. "You had no right to take that."

"I considered that typewriter my legal possession," Madame Foss said. "I took it and sold it and applied it against the rent."

"Stole it, you mean. Anyway, it was rather foolish of you. You removed his whole means of livelihood."

"He hasn't written anything in a long, long time, baby."

"He's been *sick* for a long, long time!"

"Well, he can't write when he's sick, can he?"

Linda sighed. There, she thought, was another example of Madame Foss's impregnable logic. "I'm going to the Consulate," she said.

"You can't get off this island without paying me," Madame Foss said with a bright, sweet smile. "There's blacks on this island would do anything for me. All I need to do is say the word." Then she said, "But don't worry, pet. Every cloud has its sunny side. He'll get better, he'll write something, I'll get my money, and we'll all be happy as clams at high tide." She turned to Madras. "Won't we, Madras?"

Madras nodded. Between sips from his little bottle he was munching a banana.

Madame Foss laughed. "Hey! How many swizzles you had, Madras?" she said. "Look at you! Drinking your silly head off. Oh, well, it kills the time for you, don't it, honeybunch?"

"Oh, God," Linda said softly.

"What'd you say, pet?"

"I said 'Oh, God!' " Linda said.

"Well, that's right. Prayer ought to help."

Another native girl came out on the veranda, looked at them all, giggled, and ran back inside the house.

"Wasn't that Skydrop?" Linda asked. "Did you hire her back?"

"Yes," Madame Foss said. "I forgave her."

"For*gave* her!"

"They love me, all these girls. They always come back."

"I don't see why—the way you treat them."

A week ago Skydrop had been fired for a crime that had been actually Linda's. Putting away the playing cards, after a bridge game one evening, the drawer had stuck in the writing table in the lounge and, as Linda tugged at it, the green-shaded student lamp on the table lurched and fell to the floor, shattering the globe. Linda had picked up the pieces and put them in the wastebasket, making a mental note to tell Madame Foss about it in the morning. But, coming down for breakfast, she had heard Madame Foss say to Madras, "Guess what, ducks? I had to fire that wretched Skydrop. Guess what she did. She broke my precious lampshade on the writing desk and then, when I called her in about it, the lying darky had the nerve to stand there, look me straight in the eye, and deny it! And me with all the evidence too—pieces of glass right in the wastebasket!"

Linda had said, "Oh, *no!* No, *I* broke it—last night. She was telling you the truth." Madame Foss had laughed and shrugged and said, "Oh, well, what does it matter, pet? I'll get another maid as good as her." "But that's a terrible injustice!" Linda had said. "When a maid works for thirty-five cents a day," Madame Foss had said, "we don't worry too much about *justice,* pet!"

And now, forgiven, Skydrop was back.

"Yes," Madame Foss said again, "they love me. Don't you, Heaven Hill?" Heaven Hill giggled and agreed. "Skydrop and Heaven Hill live like ladies of the land," she said. "And say," she said to Linda, "don't you think it's cute, the names I give them? They've got other names of course, lord knows what they are, but I give them pretty names like Skydrop and Heaven Hill. Pretty names for pretty girls."

Linda looked away. The woman, she thought, is insane. I am trapped here, in this terrible heat, on this awful island, with a sick husband and a crazy woman. "Madame Foss," she said softly, "I don't know what else Harry and I have got now besides our clothes, my wedding ring, a few things like that. You've got the typewriter. I'll give you my clothes—anything— if you'll lend me enough money to get Harry to San Juan."

"Oh, I wouldn't take your clothes, pet. And if I took the ring it would bring me bad luck. So don't fret."

"Oh, please, Madame Foss," she said wearily. "Please help me. I'll pay you back, I swear it."

"I *am* helping you, pet!" Madame Foss said. "Who's been paying for the French doctor to come all the way over from Basse-Terre three times a week to see him? Thirty francs already that's cost me! Who's going to pay me back for that? Have I even asked to be paid back for that?"

"You'll get it back," Linda said, "as soon as we get somewhere where we can—"

"Don't fret," Madame Foss said. "I'm not worried. But I'm no Mrs. Moneybags, though you may think so from my jewelry." She arched her fingers and looked, with a sudden smile of delight as though she had never noticed them before, at the rings they held. "Besides," she said, "your daddy's going to wire you every cent you need."

"I don't know that at all," Linda said. "I'm not at all sure he will. He hasn't answered any of my letters. And I can't even get him on the telephone."

"Your call will come through. Be patient."

"I've had that call placed for two days!"

"The phone service here is always a little slow, pet," Madame Foss said. "The cable has to handle Marie-Galante too, don't forget. Every call has to take its turn, that's the rule."

"If you knew how it kills me to sit here and beg you like this," Linda said. And then, dully, "Just two hundred dollars. That's all I need."

"Your daddy's rich. Your husband told me that."

"Did he also tell you that when we were married he cut me off without a cent?" she said. "Did he? Did he tell you I was thrown out of the house for marrying Harry?"

"Well," said Madame Foss, rocking backward and forward in her chair, "if you two was going to live with no money, that was your choice, wasn't it? Make your bed, you got to sleep in it, that's my motto. Of course," she added, "if you was going to try to live with no money, you should have had richness of spirit to make up for it. And that's what young people nowadays *lack,* if you ask me my opinion of it."

"Harry made money," she said, "when he was well! He's

only twenty-six. How were we to know that he'd—get sick?"
Suddenly she was afraid she was going to cry, and she took a
deep breath and closed her eyelids tight to hold the tears back.
I won't cry in front of her, she told herself, I won't! I'll cry
inside my head, where she can't see.

"The French doctor's coming again today," Madame Foss
said. "He'll make your Harry right as rain."

"The French doctor!" she said angrily, her eyes still pressed
tightly shut. "What kind of doctor is he! What kind of doctor
would come to this Godforsaken place! I don't think he's even
a *doctor!*"

"*What?* Why, he's the best doctor in Guadeloupe!"

"He's the *only* doctor! I can't even seem to find out his name.
He doesn't even know what Harry's got!"

"His name is some funny French name, and it's slipped my
mind," Madame Foss said primly. "You know I don't understand the lingo. We call him the French doctor here, and we
always have. What's more," she said, "he does know what your
Harry's got, and so do I."

"What is it, then?"

Madame Foss folded her hands and looked down at them.
In a different voice, she said something Linda could not hear.

"What?"

"Dysentery," Madame Foss said.

"How do you know?"

"My first husband, the captain. He had it."

"Is—was that what he died of?"

"Yes."

"And who treated him?" Linda said.

"The French doctor."

For a moment Linda wanted to say something bitter and

cruel, but then, as the bitter and cruel words swam meaninglessly in her mind, she began to wonder if she could control her tongue and lips to speak. A small, dull edge of fear had formed in her throat. The stillness and the heat of the air descended upon her and it seemed impossible to breathe. "I've got to get him to San Juan," she said at last. "Or somewhere."

"The French doctor will be here soon," Madame Foss said. "He'll fix your Harry up again as right as rain."

"Well," she said, trying to keep her voice level and matter-of-fact, "what if he doesn't? What if Harry dies? What will I do then?" She felt her voice traveling toward some thin place where, if it tripped slightly on a single syllable, it might collapse altogether. "Really—have you thought of that? What are you going to do with me?" She looked quickly away, thinking that never in her life had she stood so close to panic.

"When you first came, you told me you were adventurous types," Madame Foss said. "I thought to myself, How nice! My first husband, the captain, he was an adventurous type. That was why I thought it was nice you were staying here at Club Caprice."

"The adventure is over now," Linda said.

"Ah," said Madame Foss, shaking her orange curls, "I think it is just beginning, baby."

Yes, Linda thought, it's true. Silly as she was, a great deal of what Madame Foss said was ribbed with a kind of terrible truth; that was why she could not be argued with. Yes, they had been adventurous types. On freighters through the South Seas and to China, through the Mediterranean to Portugal, the Canaries, the West Indies . . . tropical places had been what they liked the best, the sunny islands. The attractive young couple, the young writer and his pretty wife; the pretty young woman with the handsome husband who was surely someday going to be the most famous writer in the world, they had wanted to be beachcombers, and this was what had come of it. They had combed the beaches and found—nothing.

Madras, his fingers moving very slowly, was unstoppering another of his little bottles. "How about some bridge?" Madame Foss cried suddenly. "Come on, pet—it'll ease your mind."

Weakly, Linda was grateful. "All right," she said. She rose and crossed the veranda to the bridge table. Madras pulled his chair forward, and Heaven Hill came to sit with them as a fourth.

"Put a record on the gramophone, Heaven Hill," Madame Foss said. "Play something real pretty. Play 'The Last Time I Saw Paris'—I do love that tune!"

Heaven Hill put the record on and wound up the victrola while Linda shuffled and dealt the cards.

Linda opened. "Pass," she said.

"One no-trump," said Madame Foss.

"Two clubs," said Madras, after some thought.

"Fi' diamonda!" squealed Heaven Hill.

"Six no-trump!" shouted Madame Foss, not waiting for Linda to pass. It was bidding typical of their card games because Heaven Hill and Madame Foss, who were always partners, had played for so many years together that they reached their slam contracts by an instant, psychic process. Heaven Hill laid down her cards. "Very pretty, partner," said Madame Foss.

She has us again, Linda thought, as she watched her play the hand, deftly and from old experience, drawing her trump, ruffing back and forth from her hand to the dummy, out of the dummy into her hand.

"I don't want to play any more," Madras said, standing up

when Madame Foss had collected her tricks. "It's so hot my bones ache." He went to the hammock where Linda had been sitting and lay face down upon it.

Madame Foss tapped her little stack of cards on the table. "Poor Madras," she said. "He drinks too much. The captain never drank, only beer. But," she said with her brightest smile, "at least Madras is always good as gold, and kind as kind can be to me."

There was a sound in the yard outside, and Linda looked up and saw the little French doctor coming up the path. His black bag was in one hand and he carried his shoes in the other, and he was barefoot from walking across the muddy sand dunes from the other island.

"Here he is!" cried Madame Foss. "Here's our little handsome! Come in, come in, my little precious!"

"Look . . . look," the little doctor said in his halting English, and pointed up at the sky where, Linda realized, a dark cloud had covered the sun.

"Oh, good—a storm!" said Madame Foss. "It's going to rain, and that will cool the air, and that will make our dear Harry feel so much better." And, to be sure, a cool, sharp wind blew across the veranda.

The doctor stood at the top of the steps, bowing at them. "How . . . is . . . he?" he asked. "Very well?"

Linda stood up. "He isn't very well," she said quickly. "He's not well at all, he's exactly the same. He can't eat. Can't you give him penicillin? Can't you give him something?"

"Run along upstairs, doctor," Madame Foss said, interrupting. "Run along up and fix him up. Did you get my toothbrush?"

"Oui, madame," he said, smiling and bowing again, and pro-

duced a red toothbrush in a plastic cylinder from his coat
pocket. With a deep bow, he handed it to her.

"Oh, you're an angel!" said Madame Foss. "A Dr. West, my
favorite kind—and red, my favorite color. Now run along up
to our patient."

"I brought new medicine," the doctor said, bobbing up and
down in front of Linda. "Very good, I hope."

"Yes," she said angrily. "I hope so too." She turned away
from him.

"Only you could save him, bless you," said Madame Foss.
"You're Gemini, and that gives you brains."

The doctor bowed himself through the door and into the
house, and Heaven Hill followed him, a few steps behind.

The clouds were now racing in very quickly from the east,
and the sky had grown much darker. Suddenly, with a great
explosive sound, the rain came down. Lashed by the wind, in
giant pellets, it blew in across the open porch. Madame Foss
tiptoed to Madras. "Madras?" she said. "Oh, he's dead to the
world. Should I leave him here, do you think? Oh, well, I might
as well. If he gets wet it'll cool his skin, and he'll feel better
when he wakes up." Moving about the veranda, she began clos-
ing the heavy wooden storm shutters across the windows. "My
poor husband," she said, reaching across him to close a shutter.

"Is he really your husband?" Linda asked.

"He's as good as any!" Madame Foss said sharply. "Now
don't you criticize! You know, I'll bet you're Pisces. Pisces are
always the critical types."

When they were in the house and had shut the heavy door
behind them the air was still very close and warm, but it was
full of noise now from the storm outside. The lounge was dark,
and the electric bulbs—too weak to light the room anyway—

were flickering. Linda sat down in one of the perspiring leather chairs. "Madame Foss," she said, "you've got to listen to me. I've got to get Harry off this island, and you've got to help me. Madame Foss, I don't know what you think of me, but you've got to help another human being! You must know where I can get two hundred dollars. You said your father owned the bank here."

"My father was a planter," Madame Foss said. "He was Danish, you know, and the Danish are the solid types. Now my mother, she had Gypsy blood. A stroke of the tarbrush, some said, but it wasn't true—it was Gypsy blood in her."

"You're not answering my question!"

"My father was a substantial man, as all Danes are," Madame Foss said. "But that doesn't make me a Mrs. Moneybags, my pet. I've had a slow season here," and she nodded significantly at Linda as if to say that Linda, to a large extent, had been to blame. "All I own is this hotel and the jewels the captain gave me, and I'd never part with either."

Linda sighed and lighted a cigarette. "I'm ready to give up," she said. All around the house there was the deafening pummel of the blowing rain and the slap of palm fronds against the roof and walls.

She knew all at once what she wanted of the storm. She wanted it to worsen. Sitting there in the damp, fitful wind that had crept into the room now, even through the bolted shutters, wind that stirred the heavy curtains and lifted the corners of the table doilies, riffled the pages of the old magazines that were scattered about the tables—and hearing a new sound, which was the human whispering and moaning of the native women in the kitchen who chanted against the storm and sat with their heads covered with bits of sacking and flannel to ward off the evil eye —she wanted the storm to take the house. She wanted the waves to plunge over the sea wall, leveling it, to batter against the stone walls of the hotel and rip the heavy shutters from their hinges. She would run to Harry first and lift him from his bed, and together they would be borne by the wind through the open window, into the storm, across the submerged court-yard, into the waves. She wanted the waves to sweep them, with the house, into the wild and wailing sea, and to see all of them, sobbing and screaming (except for her; she would not scream; she would smile), tossed among the floating palm fronds and debris, past the tops of trees, and out into the incalculable dark-ness beyond. Wordlessly, smoking her cigarette, she urged the sea outside to come closer, closer. . . .

But the sea was not obeying her, and the sound outside was steady and unchanged. And then, with a little gasp that was neither of fear nor of joy she realized that she had just heard the sharp ring of the telephone.

Madame Foss smiled. "There he is," she said. "Your daddy. See? I told you your call would have its turn."

"Would you answer it, Madame Foss? Please? It—it might not be he."

Madame Foss stood up and went into the little vestibule where the telephone was. When she came back her face was beaming. "It's him all right!" she said. "He's on the phone, pet!"

Linda stood up. She walked slowly into the dark little vesti-bule and closed the door behind her. She rested her cigarette on the edge of the telephone stand and sat down in the small, stiff-backed chair. The receiver lay on the table and, very care-fully, using both hands she reached for it and picked it up. She put the mouthpiece to her lips. "Hello?" she said.

An angry electric crackle answered her and, from somewhere far beyond it, a buried voice was saying unintelligible words.

"Allo?" she said. "Allo? Avez-vous mon numéro—à New York? Hello?"

Again there was only the bursting, crackling noise in her ear. She jiggled the bar up and down. "Operator?" she said. The jiggling with her finger did no good, and the phone continued to produce only forest-fire sounds. Then she heard, or thought she heard, her father's voice. "Daddy?" she cried. "Daddy, is that you?" She repeated it. "Daddy? Is that you?" And then, "Daddy, I can't hear a thing! Daddy, what did you say?" And then, "Daddy—it's Linda. It's Linda, Daddy! Oh, this is hopeless! I can't hear a thing you're saying. Daddy—please—can you hear me? Daddy, don't say anything, because I can't *hear* you! But you can hear me, can't you? Can you?" Then, in a burst, she said, "Daddy, don't go on talking because I can't hear a word! This phone just—listen, Daddy, just listen to me, if you can hear me. Oh, Daddy, I'm so scared! Daddy, perhaps I was wrong, but that doesn't matter now. Harry is very sick. Daddy, I'm afraid he's going to die! He's lost so much weight! It was something he caught on the boat, Daddy, because when we came here he was sick, and he's just kept getting worse. Nobody can— Daddy! I need a little money, Daddy. I need a little money. I've got to get him somewhere, to a doctor. To San Juan, or Miami—or even to New York if you'd send me enough money! Have you gotten my letters, Daddy? Daddy, you can't go on blaming me for this *forever!* Oh, Daddy, it's *me*—your daughter! Oh, remember . . . remember . . . oh, Daddy, please, for God's sake, you can't blame me forever! Daddy, is my mother there? Daddy, may I speak to my mother, please?" There was an exceptionally loud explosion of static in her ear, and she held the phone away, and she suddenly had a vision of the telephone lines that were strung across the island, lines that

looked so old and frayed, with their insulation hanging from
them in loops and swags and festoons—and she saw these lines
now, the festoons swaying crazily in the storm, and thought,
There are only these poor cords connecting my voice to his!
And, whether the storm that instant snapped one of the rotting
poles like a kitchen match or whether her father had simply
hung up on her, she suddenly realized that the receiver she held
was as dead and silent as a stone. She replaced the receiver
slowly in its cradle and picked up her still-lighted cigarette.

When she came back into the lounge she saw that Madras
had come in. He stood there, dripping wet, grinning at her
foolishly and rubbing his eyes.

"Well," Madame Foss said brightly, "we're all set now,
aren't we? He's sending you the money."

"Nothing is set," Linda said. "He's not sending me anything."

Madame Foss's face fell. Her mouth quivered and her eyelids puckered. "Oh, pet!" she said, and Linda thought, Why,
she really does care, after all! She cares a little, in her own way.

But then Heaven Hill came running down the stairs. "Doctor
says come quickly!" she said.

"Take a grip on yourself, baby," Madame Foss said. She
lifted herself heavily out of her chair and, in a little procession,
the four went up the stairs to Harry's room.

His face was like wax through the curtain of mosquito net-
ting, and his eyelashes were dusty with sleep and fever, and
very still.

"Harry?" she said. "Harry?"

He opened his eyes. "I wish—" he was saying.

"What do you wish, darling?"

Madame Foss went to his bedside and lifted the curtain.

"Your wish will be granted," she whispered. "The stars say it. You'll get your wish within a three."

"Within a three? Do we still owe rent?"

"You owe me no rent," Madame Foss said.

The doctor came and held Harry's wrist. Suddenly Skydrop, who had been kneeling behind the curtain, sobbed loudly and ran out of the room. Heaven Hill followed her. Linda smoothed the covers on his bed, and said, "There, there, darling."

His eyes were moving all over the room, at each of them standing there: at Madras in the corner, soaked to the skin; at Madame Foss, who was sweating and brushing the sweat away from her face with her ringed fingers all bedizened and bejeweled; then up at the little doctor, and then at last at her. "Why is everyone here?" he asked. "I'm glad to see you, Madras." Madras bowed his head.

"And you," his eyes said to her. And you. She felt the words and heard them, even though they were not spoken, and she knew what the words meant, and even the dust and the smell of chlorides and citronella and the heat and the sound of rain on the storm shutters, and the whole great stone room said it. And you, and of course you.

"My darling," she said.

She looked at Madras. Bending, leaning, stooping forward so far, with his face so slippery and wet from tears and drink, he bent so far that his steel-rimmed spectacles slipped from his nose onto the bare floor. There was a little tinkle.

It broke like glass, that moment, and she stood there feeling as though the blood were being drained out of her and was spilling, this way and that, and that bits of herself were floating away as carelessly and fortuitously as dreams slip from the mind of the dreamer. She had the feeling all at once of hearing a life break, and she put her hands down hard on Harry's shoulders to keep him from dying. And then, or maybe sooner, she knelt and placed her cheek beside him on the bed as a sort of an oblation, and she kept thinking, Why, why, why? And she looked at him and kept thinking, Why? The pestilence in the air seemed to rise around them both and fog them in like ships or statues, and she kept smelling sickness and death, sickness and death, sickness and death. The little doctor wrung his hands over her.

"Oh, he is dead, madame. Oh, he is dead."

She stood up and admitted she knew it. She had paced that strip of floor, around the island of his bed, for days, waiting, watching for a portent, a sign, for a cloud to lift. It hadn't, and she stood there now, numb and dry-eyed, waiting for grief to thunder over her.

In front of her a little parade was forming. Like ballet figures they moved across her vision—the two maids, Skydrop and Heaven Hill, and the old cook from the kitchen, and the girl who collected the washing, the little waitress, and the two little barefoot girls who gathered sticks from the beach every day for the fires, and one or two others she had barely noticed before. They moved slowly, in a column, to the bed. Then each knelt at the foot, briefly whispered something, placed a small object on the bed, rose, and moved on. They brought tiny packets tied in bits of bright cloth and handkerchiefs, and left them across the bedspread in a straight, perfect line.

Linda took Madame Foss's arm. "What are they doing?" she whispered.

"Offerings for the dead," Madame Foss said. "It's the custom."

Linda picked up one of the little knotted sacks and heard the soft chink of coins inside.

"It's money," she said. "I can't—"

"Hush," Madame Foss said. "They bring it to you. You must take it."

"I won't," she said. "I won't take money from them. Tell them to take it away."

"If you return it, the women will have a death come soon to someone they love. That is the belief."

She shook her head slowly, uncomprehendingly, back and forth. No, it was too ironic. "No, no. . . ." she said.

"Quick," Madame Foss said, "take it. They're waiting."

Slowly she reached down and picked up the little packets one by one and gathered them in her hands. She turned to the women. They faced her with downcast eyes, then turned away and filed slowly out of the room.

The rain stopped as quickly as it had begun, and the sun reappeared. Linda went downstairs and out onto the veranda outside the hotel and stood under the dripping bougainvillea vines. Madame Foss came out the door behind her and took her hand. "We are sorry," she said.

Linda said nothing.

"The women share your grief this way," Madame Foss said. "We all share it. You loved him. More than the stars."

"Please, dear," Linda said, "leave me alone for a little bit."

"How much will you need to return to your father?"

"I'm not going back to him."

"You may stay here as long as you wish."

"I can't stay here, either. Just—just leave me alone, please."

"Where will you go?"

"I don't know. Please—I want to be alone for a little while."

After a while—after Madame Foss had left—she went down the steps and started down the road toward the pier. Bright patches of water lay evaporating in the hollows of the pavement

and by the time she reached the pier every sign of the storm
was gone. She stood looking out at the sea that was as still as
death again, and pretty soon the boys from the docks were
swarming all around the young American woman, saying, "Dive
for coins, miss? Dive for coins?" She reached in the pockets
of her cotton skirt, and began undoing one after another of the
little cloth sacks. Why should anyone share my grief? she asked
herself. My grief is my own. The boys flipped like porpoises
from the pier as she tossed the coins to them.

But all the silver in the world scattered in the ocean wouldn't
bring him back. And when suddenly she saw her own pale re-
flection in that moon of blue water she too was moonlike, her
face as round, as flat, as simple, and as humble as a penny, and
she felt all at once deprived even of grief, as though grief had
been delivered to her and she had succeeded in returning grief
to its source without even once having felt its touch, and now
there was nothing in the world to do but to say good-by. And
the boys, seeing that she was out of coins, ran back and left her
there saying good-by.

ABOUT THE AUTHOR

STEPHEN BIRMINGHAM was born May 28, 1930, in Hartford, Connecticut, and was graduated in 1946 from the Hotchkiss School and in 1950 from Williams College, where he was a member of Phi Beta Kappa and co-editor of the college magazine. Mr. Birmingham has been writing since his early teens and his career has followed a time-worn path, from stories and poetry in school magazines, to writing courses, to a collection of rejection slips, to the first sale—a short story to Whit and Hallie Burnett's *Story* when he was twenty-two. Since then his stories, articles, and verse have appeared widely in magazines, including *Holiday, McCall's,* and *The Saturday Evening Post.*

In addition, he has published five novels: *Young Mr. Keefe* (1958); *Barbara Greer* (1959); *The Towers of Love* (1961); *Those Harper Women* (1964); and *Fast Start, Fast Finish* (1966). He has also published two books of nonfiction: *"Our Crowd": The Great Jewish Families of New York* (1967) and *The Right People* (1968). *Heart Troubles* is Stephen Birmingham's first published collection of short stories.